MW01229054

GOODBYE GORGEOUS

Lucius Anoraq is about to give up on a completely routine case. That is until he ends up in the wrong place at the right time and gets caught up in a murder that leads to a ring of jewel thieves, a fortune-teller, corruption, and multiple murders.

.

Goodbye Gorgeous
A Poached Parody

P.C. HATTER

Also known as Stacy Bender

Byrnas Books

This is a work of fiction. All of the characters, places, and events portrayed in this book are either products of the author's imagination or are used fictitiously.

Goodbye Gorgeous

Copyright © 2021 by Stacy Bender

All rights reserved. This book, or parts thereof, may not be reproduced in any form without permission.

Cover Design by Elizabeth Mackey
Art by Sara "Caribou" Miles

ISBN: 9798701137613

CHAPTER 1

I was on one of the not so reputable blocks of Central Avenue, looking for a female's errant husband. Word had it he was working at a three chair groomers. I never did find the runaway husband, but neither did I get paid for my time.

The late March day was warm, but the hippo staring up at the neon sign of the second floor dine and dice emporium called the Fleur-de-lis must have thought it was some sort of holiday with the way he was dressed. The guy was huge, and not just in a vertical way. The cigar in his massive hand looked more like a smoking toothpick.

Anyone who walked by gave the male a wide berth but kept an eye on him. The male was decked out in a style no one had seen for at least a decade. The gray sports jacket almost matched his skin tone, and the only thing more distracting than the yellow tie and white shoes was the golf ball buttons on the jacket. To call the guy noticeable was like saying Death Valley is just a tad bit warm.

The hippo lumbered across the sidewalk toward the double doors which covered the stairs leading to the second-floor club. The way he cased the street, I'd have thought he was planning a stickup if not for the clothes. The doors didn't even have time to close before a chameleon came flying through them, landing on the pavement in a heap between two parked cars. The lavender suited lizard picked himself up slowly from the ground, found his hat, and walked shakily up the street.

My father always said I must have been part cat

because I was always sticking my nose into things that weren't any of my business. When I poked my head through the double doors to see what was what, a huge gray hand came out of the dimness to settle on my shoulder with a crushing grip. The eyes were blank and the voice soft for such a large male. "There's scales in here."

I'd noticed the Private Club sign on the door along with the words, Lizards Only, but apparently the hippo hadn't noticed because he kept on talking. "I just threw one of them out. Did you see?"

"Yes, but what do you expect? It's a lizards only club."

"Shut your mouth. This was a respectable joint." The hippo didn't give me time to point out the sign before I felt the pressure of his fingers digging into my flesh, making me want to yelp. "Jade used to work here. Sweet little Jade, I haven't seen her in years."

The hippo lifted me up a couple of steps. Probably so that he didn't have to bend down to look me in the eye. I managed to wriggle out of his grasp and put a little room between us, my exit blocked and me without a gun. While I hadn't thought I'd need one when I'd originally set out that morning, I doubted this hippo would have noticed anything smaller than a bazooka.

"Why don't you and me go up and have a bite? I haven't seen Jade in eight years, and she hasn't written in six. But I know her, she'll have a reason."

As much as I wanted to point out that the place wouldn't serve us, I preferred all my bones unbroken more, so I nodded and bounded up the stairs. On the way, I heard the hippo say again, "Jade used to work here."

My shoulder was numb where the big male had gripped me, so I tucked my fluffy tail between my legs and bolted for the upper room.

CHAPTER 2

Another pair of swinging doors were at the top of the stairs, and I paused just long enough for the hippo to pass me and walk right through. The smart thing to do would have been to run back down the stairs and as far away as possible. No one ever said I was smart.

There were a few customers in the long narrow room. They all quieted down to gaze at us with unblinking dark eyes that had the fur on my back standing on end. Even the chatting at the crap tables stopped as the players turned their attention to us.

A thick necked crocodile wearing pink suspenders and matching arm garters slid off his barstool and sauntered over. It didn't take a genius to figure out this male was the club bouncer. "This here is a private club. No mammals allowed."

The expression on the hippo's face turned nasty as he glared at the big lizard. "Where's Jade?"

"Jade? There's no Jade here. Why don't you two run along now?"

"Jade used to work here."

The crocodile got up nice and close to the hippo, planting his large hand right on the other male's chest. "She doesn't work here now."

"Take your scaly mitts off me."

That's when the bouncer threw the first punch. It was also his last. The hippo was fast for his size but didn't move right away. The crocodile landed a perfect hit on the hippo's jaw, but he may as well have been swatting at a fly

3

for all the good it did him. The next thing anybody knew was the hippo's right hand was around the crocodile's throat and the other on his belt, and he threw the lizard across the room.

Three other lizards zipped out of the way as the male crashed into the table and slammed his head on the baseboard.

"Some males don't know when to back off," said the hippo. "Come on, friend."

Feeling awkward, I followed the lumbering behemoth to the bar and watched the patrons slowly slip out of the place. No one wanted to make any sudden moves and gain the hippo's attention. The bartender certainly didn't, but the skinny green gecko held his ground and kept wiping a glass with a bar towel.

"Whisky sour," said the hippo and motioned for me to place my order.

"Whisky sour."

The bartender made our drinks and set them in front of us when the hippo asked, "Do you know were Jade is?"

"Jade? Let me think. I've only been around here for the last year or—"

"How long's this been a place for scales?"

"Well, I…" the gecko glanced at me and looked like he was ready to faint, so I stepped in to rescue him.

"Five years. Your female wouldn't have stepped foot in this place once the new owners took over." That is, if the female was a mammal. Considering the males attitude toward lizards, I assumed she was. "No one here is going to know anything about your Jade."

"Who do you think you are?"

Angry hippos are scary to begin with. Angry with questionable mental capacity is downright terrifying. "I'm the Siberian Husky who came in with you, remember?" There are days when the ability to appear cute and fluffy comes in handy, and I gave it my all.

It worked, and the hippo calmed down and ordered

another round. Out of the corner of my eye, I spotted movement. The bouncer crawled on all fours across the floor.

"Jade did a bit of singing before this place went down the crapper. Cute little red furred thing she was. We were supposed to get married."

"Why didn't you?" I asked.

"Cause the dogs sent me up the river." The hippo jabbed a thumb into his own puffed out chest. "Me, Big Kelly, that's who I am. I did the West Bend Bank job. All by myself, forty-thousand dollars, so I didn't have to split it with nobody. Only someone stitched me up. That was eight years ago."

The sound of the crocodile fumbling with a doorknob and stumbling through distracted the hippo from whatever else he was going to say.

"Where does that go?" asked Big Kelly.

"That there goes to the manager's office," said the gecko.

"Maybe he knows where Jade is."

The gecko and I watched the hippo lumber across the floor. I'm guessing the door was locked, but that didn't matter to Big Kelly. The male ripped the door off the frame at the first sign of resistance.

When he was gone, I turned to the bartender. "That male doesn't know his own strength. Quick, what do you have back there?" When the gecko didn't answer, I added, "That male's libel to turn mean, and fast, if he doesn't get what he wants. And that's the girl he knew eight years ago. Time doesn't register with that male, get it. Please believe me when I say, I'm not with him. Never met him before today. I was just picked up off the street and dragged in here. You saw what he did to the bouncer."

"A sawed-off shotgun and a revolver."

"Okay, but let's not show our hand unless we need to. I'm not sure either of those would—"

A dull flat sound from somewhere in the building

interrupted me, and a creeping dread crawled up my spine as I slowly turned to the shattered door to the office.

Big Kelly lumbered back into the room holding a Colt Army .45 that looked like a toy in this meaty grip. "Don't move."

We didn't.

The hippo glanced around the empty place before saying, "He didn't know where Jade was," and walked out of the place.

When he was out of sight, I jumped the bar, shoved the gecko out of the way, grabbed the shotgun, and found the revolver hidden in a cigar box behind the bar. Jumping over the bar again, I bolted for the offices. The crocodile was unconscious on the floor in the hall, but the manager still sat in his chair. Only the iguana had his head folded back in a way I didn't think possible. A drawer in the desk was pulled open and the odor of gun oil tainted the crumpled newspaper inside.

After making sure the iguana was dead, I locked the office door, set the guns down, and used the telephone on the desk to call the police.

CHAPTER 3

A Doberman by the name of Denson caught the case, and not the kind with a nice physique. This one ate too many treats and didn't get enough exercise. The dog was a detective lieutenant attached to the 77th Street Division. We sat in a room so crowded with desks and chairs, you couldn't wag a tail.

"Nearly twenty years in the police force and this is what I get." The Doberman picked up my card and read it again. "Lucius Anoraq, Private Investigator. Okay blue-eyes, what were you doing in a lizards only club? Particularly what you were doing while the manager of said club was getting his head twisted off."

"Talking to the bartender."

"What bartender? You were in the office with the corpse when we found you. Don't you carry a gun?"

"I know, I called it in. As for a gun, errant husband cases usually don't require me to carry one." I held up my hand to keep him from asking more questions. "Let me start from the beginning. The case I was on took me to the groomers across the street. That's when I saw the hippo and got curious. Not only did the male throw lizards around, but he nabbed me and decided I'd make a good drinking buddy."

"At gun point?"

"No, I think he took the gun off the manager who I'm guessing tried to shoot him. But let's face it, no one wanted to argue with the guy, and those that did came to a bad end. Though I didn't think he'd kill anyone, he certainly didn't know his own strength. No, that hippo was dressed to meet someone, not kill them."

"Who was he wanting to meet?"

"A dame, what else. Apparently, she worked at the Fleur-de-lis as a singer before Big Kelly pulled the bank job that put him behind bars. If you find Jade, you'll probably find Big Kelly."

Denson barked a laugh. "Yeah, when I'm on my third set of teeth. No one cares about this neighborhood. Even the journalists don't bother coming around here anymore. Not enough glamor."

"Perhaps he's skipped parole? You could get help from them. But whatever you do, be careful when you grab him, or he'll put all your dogs in the hospital."

"And if that happens, they'll give the case to someone else. I'm too low in the pack to warrant any press worthy cases." The telephone on his desk rang, and he picked it up. After listening to the person on the other end and scratching down some notes, he hung up and looked at me. "That was records. They got a file on him. At least that's something."

"Are you going to find the female?"

"Me, in a joy house? That's a laugh." The Doberman sobered and looked at me. "I checked up on you. Seems you could use a friend on the force."

"Don't tell me you're willing to pay me to find this dame."

"No, nothing like that. It's just… Well, if you do find something." The dog shrugged and looked away.

"If I stumble across something, I'll give you a howl. But right now, I need some lunch. Don't worry, you'll get the hippo. He's too big to miss." I grabbed my hat, said goodbye, and headed across the street for something to eat.

The case wasn't any of my business, but not only was I curious, I was bored. With no paying cases to work on, I didn't have anything to distract me from snooping.

CHAPTER 4

The Fleur-de-lis was closed up with a patrol car camped out front. With the manager, who was also the owner, dead and the bouncer and bartender in the wind, it was useless. A dead-end, really. Neither males would have any information.

I parked my car and studied the street before taking a chance with the hotel that sat diagonally from the club. By the number of warming rocks in the lobby, it was obvious the place catered to lizards. The bearded dragon behind the desk looked like he was sleeping. His eyes were closed, and his hands were flat on the counter, but otherwise his suit was impeccable.

By the time I walked up to the counter, the lizard's eyelids were half open and looking at me.

"Hi there, the names Lucius Anoraq. Have you heard about the trouble across the street?"

"Trouble?"

Lizards are notoriously difficult to read, but at the darkening of this one's scales, I figured I had his attention. I pulled a half-dollar coin out of my pocket and spun it on the counter like a top.

"Yes, the manager got bumped off," I said.

"May he rest with the angels." The lizard's eyes slid from the spinning coin back up to my face. "Are you a cop?"

"Private investigator."

The ability to wait out a lizard requires patience, and then some. I'd almost given in when he asked, "What happened?"

"A very large and very mad hippo is what happened.

Seemed the guy got out of the joint and set off looking for his female. Only when he got to Fleur-de-lis where she used to work, she was gone, and the place had changed hands."

The coin stopped spinning and fell with a ringing whirr onto the counter, but still there was no reaction from the lizard.

"Perhaps I could buy you a drink?" I pulled the bottle from my pocket.

This time I got a smile, and after a quick glance around he said, "Why don't you come over to the side of the desk?"

I did as instructed. The lizard gathered two glasses and did the pouring. He must have known his liquor because after tasting it, he gave me an even bigger smile.

Once I gave him the complete rundown of what happened across the way, the bearded lizard's scales brightened, but he looked solemn. "Poor male. Louie kept a nice quiet place and didn't tolerate no funny business. Shame he's dead."

"Do you remember what the name of the place was before he took over? Or for that matter, the name of the previous owner?"

"The place changed hands, but the name stayed the same. Electric signs are expensive. As for the original owner, that would be Andy Bloom. And that rat died in 1934, or was it 35? I don't rightly remember, but he pickled his organs right good."

"Any relatives?"

"Just his wife." The lizard corked the bottle and handed it back to me. "Her name's Ginger." He then pulled a heavy directory out from somewhere beneath the desk and let me flip through it. When I found the name, he handed me paper and pen to write the address down, and the big book went back underneath the desk.

While I walked out the door, he settled back to his sleepy position.

CHAPTER 5

The address for Ginger Bloom wasn't what I was expecting. While the neighborhood seemed nice, Mrs. Bloom's house didn't live up to her last name. Even the weeds had trouble growing in her yard, and the few that tried were brown and brittle.

I parked the car, walked up to the house, and had to knock because the doorbell didn't work.

When the female did come to the door, the boney rat wore a stained and faded bathrobe. My fingers itched to check on my flea collar, but I managed to resist.

"Mrs. Bloom? Mrs. Ginger Bloom? Wife of Andy Bloom who owned Fleur-de-lis?"

"Yeah." She shuffled forward and looked up at me with bleak watery eyes until my words slowly registered. "Andy's been gone five years now. Bastard left me penniless."

"I'm a private detective, ma'am, and I'm looking for information."

"Then you best come in." She unhooked the latch of the screen and let me inside. "I haven't had time to clean up yet."

I stepped through the door, half expecting a trash pile. While everything was old and worn and near collapse, actual trash was kept to a minimum while a thick layer of dust covered most surfaces. The only thing of value in the place was the large cabinet radio that stood to the left of the door and emitted music. Unlike everything else, the thing wasn't just new, but had no dust on its surface.

Mrs. Bloom sat in a rocking chair, but while I attempted to sit in an overstuffed chair, I had to remove the empty gin bottle to do so.

"I doubt Andy's done anything lately on account of being dead, so what brings you here?"

"Someone with red fur named Jade. I don't have a last name, but she probably used a stage name. The place on Central is a private club now, and they wouldn't know anything about her, so I came to you."

"Why are you looking for her?"

"Her folks want to find her. An inheritance is involved and where money is concerned, people get particular."

The rat licked her lips and asked, "Do you got anything to drink, or do you being a cop prevent that?"

Since I still had most of the bottle from earlier, I pulled it out but kept it in my hand.

"You aren't a cop." While she said the words, her eyes locked onto the bottle. She panted with excitement before licking her lips. The thirst for alcohol would win in the end.

"Jade was a torch singer, I believe. Perhaps you knew her? That is, if you were down there much."

"Glasses, we need glasses." The rat scurried out of the room and came back with two dirty glasses. I filled hers but kept mine to a minimum and hoped the alcohol sterilized the glass.

The rat downed her drink like it was nothing and held the glass out for more. "Nice stuff." She settled back after I filled her glass again. "What you want to know about?"

"Jade, a red furred female that used to work at the Fleur-de-lis. You were going to tell me about her."

"What's your name again?"

I pulled my card out and handed it to her. Only she didn't start talking until her third drink.

"Jade had a nice voice, but even nicer legs. That's what most males wanted to see. On stage and off. Don't know what that tramp got up to, but I don't care what any of them did as long as it kept the customers coming in and spending money."

Mrs. Bloom gave me a suspicious look, but when I acted like I was drinking, she seemed satisfied.

"Where's her folks from?"

"Their around."

After the fourth glass, she stood on wobbly legs. "I got me an idea." She staggered out of the room, and I listened to her bumping around somewhere in the house. When I heard a crashing noise followed by curses, I headed over to investigate.

Staying in the hall and careful not to let her see me, I glanced around the shambles she'd made of the back room. Drawers were pulled out, stuff knocked over, and closets opened. The rat was on her knees in front of a large chest. I watched as she dug around in the thing, drunkenly tossing items until she came up with a packet tied with a red ribbon.

She fumbled with the bow, flipped through the papers, and removed an item. That one item she shoved back into the right side of the chest before retying the ribbon and staggering to her feet.

I bolted back to the living room and acted like I'd been waiting there all along.

When the rat came back, she dropped the tied package in my lap, poured herself another drink, and dropped back into the rocking chair. "Take a look. She might be in there."

The package contained photos and newspaper clippings. I flipped through them while Mrs. Bloom complained about the tramp her old male ran after and that he hadn't left her anything. She stopped when I asked, "What am I looking for?"

"What? Don't you have a picture of her? Didn't her folks give you one?"

"No." The rat didn't like that, but her brain was too drowned in alcohol to think very fast. I stood, set the bottle next to her, and asked, "Pour me one before you finish the bottle."

Before she could do anything else, I bolted down the hall to the chest, and pulled out the envelope she'd tried to hide. When I got back to the living room she was standing, though barely. "Damn copper. I'll—"

"Quiet," I barked. "Unlike Big Kelly, I'm no simpleton."

"Kelly?" The rat's demeanor changed at the mention of his name, and she looked around as if trying to find a place to hide. "What do you know about Kelly?"

"The hippo's out of prison and looking for Jade and the guy who yapped to the cops about him. Only now he's wandering around with a .45 after killing a lizard who couldn't give him the answer he wanted, and the cops are after him."

This time when she took a drink, she didn't bother to use a glass.

I opened the envelope and found a professional photo of a female fox in a Pierrot costume from the waist up. Since the photo was black and white, I couldn't tell if she was red furred, but the signature was a Jade Rose. In profile, the female had a pretty face under the conical hat, but not the Hollywood silver screen type. She was more the average seen all over town type.

"Why'd you hide Jade's picture, Mrs. Bloom? Where is she?"

"She's dead, been dead. Now go away."

"When did she die?"

Instead of answering the question, she gave me a string of curses that could strip the paint off a car. Tucking the photo into my pocket, I left for the front door and barely missed the now empty liquor bottle she tried tossing at my head.

On my way out to the car, I spotted the curtains move in the house next door and noted the nosey neighbor. Instead of talking to them, I climbed back into my car and drove back to Denson's tiny office.

CHAPTER 6

Denson didn't appear to have moved when I got to his office, other than to light another cigar. The Doberman handed me a photo when I sat down. "Recognize him?" It was Big Kelly's mug shot.

"That's him."

"Someone spotted him on the Seventh Street line, and he got off at Third and Alexandria. There's lots of big empty houses downtown that no one wants to live in. We'll get him when he breaks into one of those."

"Was the hippo wearing a fancy hat and golf balls on his shirt? Because if not, you're chasing the wrong hippo." I waited for Denson to double-check the paperwork and could read the disappointment in his eyes. "That's right, Big Kelly was just that, big. He's not the type of hippo that can buy stock sizes and have them fit properly."

Denson let out a growl and chewed his cigar. "So, what have you been doing?"

"Nothing much, I just talked to one of the staff at a hotel across the street from the club. The current and now deceased owner never changed the name of the place because the sign was nice and expensive. Andy Bloom, the male he bought the place off of, is also now dead, and the widow is doing a good job of pickling her innards."

As I talked, I wrote down the widow's address and handed it to him.

"Her name is Ginger. Lovely rat, I don't think she's washed her fur since the Coolidge administration. What was more interesting is that the rat had a brand-new radio worth around seventy-five dollars sitting in her living room. Plus, she knew who Jade was and tried to hide her photo."

I handed Denson the picture I got off the widow, and he looked at it with appreciation. "Nice legs."

"It took a good bottle of bourbon to get that. Ginger Bloom said the vixen's dead, but I'm not so sure I believe her. Why hide the photo of a dead female? When I mentioned Big Kelly, the rat clammed up."

"So now what?"

"That ball is now in your court. But I am curious about the bank job. Who got the reward for squealing on the hippo?"

"Not sure, why?"

"I'm not doing your job for you unless I get paid, Denson. Think about it. The hippo gets out of jail, and one of the first things he does is go searching for his female. Don't you think he'll also want to find the person who stitched him up as well?"

I got up from the chair and said, "I'm tired from dealing with Ginger Bloom. I need a flea bath."

"How much did the old rat slip you to give this case a rest?"

It took a moment for the dog's words to register, and I bared my teeth. "Like I said, I'm not getting paid to do your job."

CHAPTER 7

The telephone on my desk rang. When I answered, the voice on the other end sounded cool yet arrogant. "This is Lucius Anoraq, isn't it? And you're a private detective, yes?"

"It is, and I am."

"You come recommended as a person who can keep their mouth shut. Seven o'clock my house, we can go over the details here. The name's Cedrick, Cedrick Brinkman." The guy on the other end of the line rattled off an address out in Montemar Vista, then told me an easier way to get to the place was to park my car at a café and walk up a set of steps.

"Mind if I ask as to the nature of the business and its legality?"

"It's legal, but it's something I have no wish to discuss over the phone. Don't worry, I'll pay you for your time and expenses."

I agreed, and after a few other details were discussed, I hung up. A paying customer would keep me afloat, even if they were treating their situation like a Hollywood script.

The second call was from Denson. "You were right. It was the wrong hippo. While we were distracted with that, Big Kelly went to see Mrs. Bloom. We got the call from the nosey neighbor next door. Two males came by to see the rat today. From the descriptions, the first was you, but the second matched Big Kelly. The only reason we got the call was that the hippo was playing with a colt, and the old bird saw him and panicked."

"Did she get the license number of the car he was driving?"

"No, her eyesight's been deteriorating, and she can't see too far away anymore. Plus, the hippo only stayed five minutes. Anyway, when the prowl boys came by to check the house, the rat was gone, so they checked in with the neighbor. They said she was fit to be tied when the bird found out Mrs. Bloom slipped out of the house without her seeing. Though when the rat came back, the bird called up again to let us know."

"I'm not surprised Big Kelly showed up at the rat's place," I said. "He probably figured the police were wise to Mrs. Bloom, and that's why he didn't stay long."

"Well, we got another line on him. He was on Girard, heading north in a rented hack. The service station attendant recognized him from the description we sent out earlier. Everything matched, only he changed to a dark suit."

"Well, good luck."

"Luck? Don't you want to join the party?"

"No thanks, I've got a paying gig to go to tonight. I took the job right before your call."

Denson let out a whine and tried keeping me interested in the case, but I declined. Paying the bills was more important.

CHAPTER 8

By the time I got down to Montemar Vista, the light was beginning to fade, but the waves of the Pacific could still be seen past the yacht harbor at Bay City. The various houses of Montemar Vista all looked like they were hanging on to the spur of the mountain by their claw tips.

I parked at the café as instructed and walked the two hundred and eighty steps up to Cabrillo Street. To say I was winded was an understatement. Only one house stood on Cabrillo Street, and I could see the huge black car in the garage. The vehicle must have cost more than the house.

When I knocked on the door, an elegantly dressed Afghan hound answered. The hound looked me up and down, but while there might have been some interest, my suit wasn't expensive enough for him. "Yes?"

"You said to be here at seven."

"Oh, yes. Please, come in, Mr." His words trailed off as he acted like my name was on the tip of his tongue.

"Lucius Anoraq," I said.

He responded by looking annoyed. "Yes, well, do come in. My house cub is away for the evening." The dog then led me into the airy space of the house that came straight off a movie set and dripped with elegance and money. Mr. Cedrick Brinkman arranged himself against the grand piano and smoothed back his long silky dark locks. "Do you carry a gun?"

"Sometimes, if the case warrants it."

"You shouldn't need it tonight. This is just a business transaction."

"Blackmail?"

Brinkman frowned again and stuck his nose in the air. "Certainly not. I've nothing to hide, and there's no reason anyone would wish to blackmail me. No, I'm meeting these males tonight, probably in some lonely out of the way place. I don't know yet, but wherever it is, it should be reasonably close. It took until today to come to an agreement."

"So, I'm playing bodyguard?"

"I'm not much of a hero, and I hadn't decided on having someone with me until this afternoon. Technically, I'm working for a friend and don't feel comfortable with so much of someone else's money in my possession."

"What's the money for, and what's the amount?"

"I'm not at liberty to say."

The job stunk, and the drama only made it worse. "So, you want me to play bodyguard without a gun, not knowing a thing about what to do or what's going on and risk my neck over something you're not going to tell me. How much is this gig worth?"

The hound shrugged. "I hadn't really thought that far ahead."

"Do you plan on figuring that out soon, or should I just leave now?"

When he didn't answer, I crammed my hat onto my head and walked toward the door.

"Wait, I'll offer you one-hundred dollars. That should be sufficient for a few hours of your time." When I stopped, but didn't say anything, he continued. "There's really no risk. My friend lost some jewelry in a hold up, and I'm buying it back is all."

I turned around and said, "Tell me about the heist."

There was another elegant shrug before the hound said, "Fei Tsui jade is very rare, and very expensive. The necklace is priceless, and while the insurance company would pay out, she'd rather have the necklace back. We were driving back from Trocadero when we had an accident. Well, really not an accident, the car just brushed the fender. When the driver stopped in front of us, it wasn't to apologize. I think there were at least three or four males, all armed."

Brinkman brushed at the silky strands that had fallen out of place before continuing.

"They took all her jewelry, the necklace included, but gave back one of her rings saying not to contact the police or insurance company. That they would be in touch with a ransom agreement. Eight-thousand dollars is rather cheap when you consider the real value of the piece, so she agreed."

"What's the lady's name?"

"That, I don't think I'll tell you," he said.

"What about the arrangements?"

Something flickered in the hound's eyes, but I wasn't sure if it was fear or not. He was a good actor because he didn't let his ears or tail give himself away. "I'm waiting for the last call."

"Did you at least mark the money?" When he made a disgusted face, I sighed and explained. "I don't mean peeing on it. I'm talking about using ink that shows up under ultra-violet light. The police use it to track criminals in situations like this."

"Oh, no. I don't know anything about things like that. Well there's no time to bother with that now. I was thinking you could hide in the back seat of my car while I made the transaction and—"

"Do you even know what you're doing, Mr. Brinkman? But more to the point, who recommended me?"

The hound had the good sense to look embarrassed before saying, "I pulled your name out of the phone book."

"Lovely. Mind if I handle the arrangements then? You can hide in the backseat. We're about the same height, so with any luck, I'll be mistaken for you." Maybe if the guy got a perm, but I wasn't going to play peek-a-boo with this

21

nut. "You do realize that there's no guarantee the thieves won't double-cross you, right? They might even knock you upside the head."

"To tell you the truth, that's what I'm afraid of, and that's why I called you."

"Tell me, did the guys shine a light in your face during the holdup?"

"No, should they have?"

I shook my head. "It was just a thought. They've had plenty of time to look you over since. Do you go out with this female much, or is she married?"

"If you don't mind, I'd like to leave her out of this."

"Fine, but you do realize that other than keeping you company, there's not a darn thing I can do if these guys decide to go off script."

"That's fine."

What I should have done was walk away from the whole affair, but a hundred dollars could go a long way. "If you don't mind, I'd like to get paid now instead of later."

CHAPTER 9

The top shelf Martell he served made the wait bearable, though we both jumped when the telephone rang the first time. From the sound of Brinkman's voice, it was a female calling. The second call was the one we were waiting for.

When the hound hung up the telephone he said, "Showtime."

"Where are we headed?"

"Purissima Canyon. Don't worry, I know the area. It's just north of Bay City." Moving like a dancer, the Afghan hound retrieved a map and showed me the area in question. I had a vague notion of where the place was. He handed me his white overcoat, but I wore my own hat. I wasn't about to let him know I'd brought a gun to the party. As for the eight grand, it felt like a brick in my pocket.

We climbed into the car and headed out. The car virtually drove itself as the engine purred, and by the time we passed the café where my car was parked, I understood why Brinkman told me to use the stairs to find his place. If a person didn't know the roads, they may as well have been traveling a maze.

Brinkman kept his head low as he peered over the seat. "Those lights over there should be the beach club. If you turn right at the second rise that will be Purissima Canyon."

I followed his directions, and the houses became fewer and far between. Even the pavement disappeared, replaced by a hard packed dirt road. We finally stopped at a white painted barrier with an opening too small for the huge car to pass through without ruining the paint job.

"Stay here," I said, and exited the car. The scent of sage filled the air, and I sneezed as I followed the road beyond the barrier where someone had hacked the bushes back in order to get through. Straining my ears to hear, I sniffed the air but came up with nothing but chirping insects and smelly plant life.

The lights of the beach club across the way shown in the darkness, and I wondered if someone was using its vantage point to keep a look out. Someone nocturnal or using night glasses would have a nice view from the upper floors of the landscape below.

After a while, I headed back to the car and put my foot on the running board. "Guess they decided to make this a trial run to see if you'd follow directions." I kept my voice low enough so that only Brinkman could hear me in the backseat.

He didn't answer, but when I stepped away from the car, someone knocked me on the back of my head.

CHAPTER 10

When I opened my eyes, I was lying on my back and felt sick as I rolled over. The pain at the back of my head traveled right down to my feet. "How long have I been out? Four minutes, possibly six?" I was talking to air, and my voice didn't sound right to my own ears as I tried figuring out what happened. "Where's Brinkman? Did he faint at the sight of the thugs or was there a gun? How were they tipped off?"

Once I managed to get to my knees, I could only think of one word to sum everything up. "Stupid."

I felt the pockets of my coat and wasn't surprised at finding the envelope missing. What was interesting was my gun was still holstered and my wallet still in my pocket. I took my hat off and felt the growing lump on the back of my head. I was going to have a splitting headache.

The florescent dial on my watch said four minutes to eleven. When Brinkman got the call, it was eight minutes after ten. While I worked out the timing between leaving the Brinkman's place and me getting sapped, the night sounds carried on as if nothing had happened. The overwhelming scent of sage made me gag. It must have been enough to cover their scent. I'd been out for about twenty minutes.

When I got to my feet and turned around, the big boat of a car was nowhere to be seen. Walking over to where the car had been, I pulled out a pocket flashlight and shined it on the ground. From there, I followed the tire tracks past the barrier and down the curving road. The ground was softer, making the tracks easier to see, but it didn't matter. Between the chromium paint and the reflectors, the car was easy enough to spot. Only it was empty, and I couldn't smell any blood inside.

The sound of a car motor from beyond the barrier had me on alert with my gun in hand, and I used the car to hide behind as the beam of headlights swept the bush. The car stopped about two-thirds of the way down, shown a spotlight over an area then continued the rest of the way.

I stayed behind the car as a flashlight scanned the area.

"Hands up and step away from the car." The voice was female, but I didn't move. "I've got ten shots that say you'd better move."

She said a few more things before I realized she was just as scared as I was. I tucked my gun away, straightened, and walked toward the light until I was six feet away and stopped.

"Who are you?" she asked.

"You talk too much when you're scared."

"I'm asking the questions."

"The names Lucius Anoraq. Do you mind getting that light out of my face?"

"Sorry. Is that your car?"

"No, my employer. Are you the dame who owns the necklace?"

"What necklace?"

My head still hurt, but I really didn't feel like playing twenty questions. "If you really do have a gun, do you mind putting it away? I've already been sapped, and I don't feel like getting shot tonight."

"You're doing better than your friend."

"Excuse me?"

"There's a dog up the road, Afghan hound possibly, with his face all bloodied it's hard to tell."

"Show me, he might still be alive." I walked forward ignoring the bobbing light.

"Are you crazy? I did say I had a gun."

"Show me."

The light of her flashlight shone briefly on a small Colt vest pocket automatic."

"Not your peashooter, the body."

"Fine, this way." She lit the way up the road and stopped before the body. I missed him because I was too focused on the tires, along with the strong scent of sage up my nose. Cedrick Brinkman was beaten to a pulp and dumped in the brush.

CHAPTER 11

"Give me the flashlight."

She handed it over, and I check Brinkman over. He was dead all right.

I swung the light back on the female. An Irish Setter mix, she didn't seem like a female who'd wear a priceless necklace. Too wholesome. She still pointed the gun at me.

"Would you mind putting that gun away and holding the light, so I can search his pockets?"

"You should wait for the police."

"Between them, the photographers, the coroner, and the guy who takes the fingerprints it'll be a while. We're nowhere near a telephone, so would you mind?"

She wavered a minute then I heard the snap of a purse, and she took hold of the light.

Brinkman carried both silver and bills in his pocket along with a small pocketknife and a leather key case. His billfold held more currency along with an insurance card, a driver's license, and receipts. In his coat, I found handkerchiefs, match folders, a gold pencil, and two different cigarette cases. The enameled one held the brown South American brand I'd seen him smoking while we were waiting back at the house. The embroidered one held oversized Russian cigarettes. Three in all, they looked old and dry.

"He must have kept these for a female friend. I saw him smoke the others."

"Don't you know for sure?"

"I only met the guy a few hours ago. He hired me as a

bodyguard."

"Some bodyguard."

"Rub it in why don't you."

"Sorry," she said. "Mind if I look at those? I bet they're jujus or something like it. Sometimes felines roll their catnip into cigarettes."

I handed her the embroidered case and turned back to the body. "Hold the light steady."

"Hang on a minute." She jiggled some more, and she tapped the case on my shoulder to let me know she was done with it, so I could put it back. "These were high-class thugs; they only took the ransom." Just to be sure, I double checked my own wallet and let the dog see my ID card.

"You know who I am, mind telling me who you are, and why you're here?"

"Mary Abrams, orphan, and single. I tend to get restless and go driving around, and since I know this neighborhood very well, I got curious. Since I also write feature articles, following my instincts helps me find good stories."

"So, you like taking risks. Does it pay well?"

"Not really. What were you looking for in his pockets?"

"Answers. Like I said, Brinkman hired me to play bodyguard. Only he didn't want to tell me much of anything. Eight-thousand dollars was supposed to buy back a fancy necklace. Why they killed the hound, I have no idea. We were supposed to drive past the barricade, but the car was too big. My guess is that while I was waiting down in the hollow, they were dealing with him back at the car. One of them must have took his place in the backseat and knocked me out when he had the chance."

"You didn't notice a smell difference?"

"People do use deodorant you know. Besides, sage is the only thing I can smell out here." I ended up sneezing, but not for emphasis. "The only reason I took this loopy job was because I needed the money. Now I'll have to deal with the cops. Could you drive me to Montemar Vista? Not only did Brinkman live there, but my car's there as well."

"Shouldn't one of us stay with the body?"

"No. I'll deal with this."

"Are you trying to be chivalrous?"

Chivalry had nothing to do with it, and though I didn't want to admit it, more to do with a dead sibling. Only I didn't want to dwell on past failings. Even the ones beyond my control.

"Just let me do this my way, okay."

She nodded, and we headed back down the hill to climb into her car. Once on the paved road she said, "How about we go back to my place. You could have a drink and relax while we wait for the police. They have to drive in from Los Angeles, anyway."

"I'll go it alone."

"But—"

"You don't need to be involved."

The dog gave me a sideways glance and kept quiet all the way to the café where I'd left my car. The place was lit up like a Christmas tree. Before I got out of her car, I handed her one of my cards. "Just in case you ever need a hand."

She took the card, smiled, and said, "819 Twenty-Fifth Street, Bay City. My numbers in the phone book."

I watched the taillights of her car disappear before getting into my own. The thought of a drink sounded nice, but I needed what little wits I had left.

Twenty minutes later, I walked into the West Los Angeles police station.

CHAPTER 12

It was well after midnight when they brought the drunk in and put him in a cell. We could hear him howling all the way into the captain's room where me, Lieutenant Hartman, and two Dingoes sat. Brinkman's body had already been found and dealt with, and I'd told my story for the fourth time.

The stuff from Brinkman's pockets filled the table. Hartman was an armadillo from Central Homicide in Los Angeles. "The more I hear this story the crazier it sounds. Why go through all that trouble in planning then hire you at the last minute as a bodyguard?"

"Guess he wanted someone to hold his hand. I didn't tell him I had a gun on me. I'm not even sure how he picked me. First, he said a friend recommended me then it was out of the phone book. I know he wasn't telling me everything, but a job's a job."

Hartman pushed a smudged business card across the table. It was one of mine. Brinkman keeping a filthy card seemed out of character. "This was in his wallet."

"I pass those out all over the place. They make good advertisements."

"Eight-thousand dollars is a lot of money to be trusted with. Are you sure that's how much there was?"

"That's what he said was in the envelope, and like I said, I'm not sure if it was his or the lady's he was buying the necklace back for. Please don't ask me again who she was because he wouldn't tell me."

"If it was hers, do you think he intended to steal the

31

money?"

The surprised look on my face must have been comical, because what came out of Hartman's mouth was laughable.

"Maybe this Brinkman fella played you, and you were supposed to be the fall guy for the cash."

"And after knocking me out, he beats himself to death?" I asked. "How did he get away with the money?"

"The hound could have had an accomplice, and both of you were supposed to be knocked out. Only the accomplice decides he doesn't want to share. And it didn't have to be the accomplice that sapped you. Brinkman could have seen the bulge in your pocket, figured you had a gun, and knocked you out. It's no sillier than the story you're telling me."

"True, but don't you think it's more likely that Brinkman knew one of the crooks, and that's why they killed him? I didn't hear anything, but that doesn't mean that they didn't come in fast or do something to keep the hound quiet."

"It was dark."

"There's still sound and smell. Maybe someone liked a particular cologne?" I rubbed my muzzle, but it was going to take a long shower for me to be able to smell much of anything again.

"Did you smell anything?"

"Sage, sage, and more sage."

The armadillo tapped his nails on the desk as he chewed his lip. "If this was a group of professional jewel thieves, they wouldn't resort to murder. Not without reason."

"That's what I was thinking."

"How'd you get from there to here?"

"Hitchhiked back to my car and drove here. The car was a Chevy coupe, didn't think about taking the license number down, but the female who was driving seemed nice enough. Irish Setter mix, I think."

Hartman glared at me. "A lone female picked you up in the middle of the night?"

"It's the eyes. Everybody loves my blue eyes."

"This is now a police case, understand. You're to stay out of it."

"No problem, I don't want it, anyway. Can I go home now, I'm not feeling all that great."

"Yes, you can go."

Before I got to the door, Hartman asked, "Do you know what kind of cigarettes Brinkman smoked?"

"Some brown South American brand. He had them in an enameled case."

"What about this case?" Hartman held up the embroidered case.

"If you're asking if I searched the body, yes. Did I disturb anything, no. The hound was a client after all."

Hartman opened the case. It was empty. "Did you ever see him smoke anything out of this one? There was powder residue in it. I'm guessing some illegal substance."

"Sorry, the only time I saw that case was when I searched him. But if he had something, I would have thought he'd have smoked them right then and there just to mellow him out."

"Goodbye, Mr. Anoraq," he said, and snapped the case closed.

I left the building wishing the bars were still open so that I could have a drink.

CHAPTER 13

The next morning, I showered, dressed, had extra coffee, and read the newspaper with my breakfast. An article about Big Kelly was on page three along with his picture, but Denson wasn't even mentioned. As for Cedrick Brinkman, his name was absent though it might have made the society papers.

The telephone rang, and when I answered it, Denson was on the other end. "Good morning Anoraq. Guess what happened on the Ventura line?"

"You took down a dangerous hippo."

"We did, only he turned out to be a very drunk male with a family."

"How embarrassing."

"We still hauled him in for assaulting a police officer, malicious damage, disturbing the peace, and a few other things. The guy was no angel, but he wasn't Big Kelly. What are you up to?"

"Nursing a headache."

"If you—"

"No. Now if you don't mind, I need to go to the office and wait for a paying job."

We said our goodbyes, and I headed for the office.

When I got there, the Irish Setter mix was waiting for me in the tiny reception area. With it being daylight, I got a much better view of her, and her outfit of conservative professional.

"Your secretary isn't in yet," she said.

"I don't have one." After unlocking the door to my

inner office, I waved her inside.

Once she got a good look at the old furniture and dusty cabinets, she sat down. "Don't you need someone to answer calls and do the paperwork?"

"I might miss a few calls, but it works for me."

"So, what happened last night? How were the police? Were they nice to you? How's your head?"

"It was all right, as for my head, it's still attached to my shoulders. If you're wondering, I managed to keep you out of it. It's a police case now, and I've been warned off."

Mary Abrams gave me a big smile. "You're so sweet. You just thought the police wouldn't believe me about driving around and were afraid they'd grill me, thinking I'd hit you over the head. Or was it because you think I'm beautiful? Do you make a lot of money in this job?"

The fast change in subject had me wondering what she was up too, but her wagging tail only indicated her level of excitement.

"I do okay."

"Would you like to know who owns the jade necklace?"

That got me. "Who said anything about the necklace being jade?"

Her tail wagged faster and her smile widened. "Blame it on the bloodhound in me. My father was the police chief of Bay City for several years, before a gambler by the name of Mike Castle managed to elect his preferred mayor. That mayor then booted my father down to the records department. Both of my parents have passed away now, but I'm still on good terms with several officers. Hartman wasn't too happy with you not telling him about me, but it's not like I said anything to you about my connections."

While she lit a cigarette, I pulled a bottle out of the desk drawer and poured myself a drink to sooth my stomach.

"Aren't you going to offer me one?" she asked.

"It's a little early, and you don't look the type."

"I'll take that as a compliment." She propped her elbows on the edge of my desk and placed her head in her hands. "From the description of that necklace, it should be a museum piece. The jeweler I talked to was very nice and informative when I told him I was a journalist working on an article. And get this, the owner of the necklace lives in Bay City. Mrs. Athena Anne French has oodles of money, something like twenty million because her husband is an investment banker. He used to own a radio station in Beverly Hills, and that's where they met. She married him five years ago, but while Mr. French is an elder tod, Mrs. Athena Anne French is a beautiful Sechuran vixen. Though, I think she gets her markings altered at the groomers. No one's that flawless without help."

"You got all this information from a jeweler?"

"Of course not, silly. I talked to the society editor of the Chronicle. I've known Bing for years. He's such an adorable Fennec, but he does have a bit of a weight problem."

She reached into her bag, pulled out a stack of photos, and arranged them on my desk. It was a fox all right, and from the look of the admiring males in some the shots, the pictures didn't do her justice.

"Nice, but what does this have to do with me?"

"Don't you want to see her? About the necklace. I've already called her up, and she said she'd see you."

"How—"

"It wasn't easy. When I finally got hold of her and mentioned Fei Tsui jade and that I was working for you, that's when I asked her if she had a private line on which to talk, and she said yes. Only she wouldn't give me the number until I asked her if she wanted her necklace back. That's when I told her all about you and what happened."

I held up a hand to halt the barrage and asked, "Does Hartman know this information?"

"Yes, I've already told him. Anyway, I have an appointment to see Mrs. French at two, and I just know she'll want to hire you."

"But I'm off the case as decreed by Lieutenant Hartman."

"If Mrs. French hires you, he can't do a thing about it. What was Mr. Brinkman like? Was he reputable?"

I didn't know what to say and ended up rubbing my temples to keep a headache at bay. "The necklace is probably at the bottom of the ocean by now along with whoever killed Brinkman. His murder was a mistake. Whoever did it was probably an overexcited pup or cub with more adrenaline than brains. If by chance the thieves know the value of the jade, that necklace won't see the light of day for years."

When I stopped talking and opened my eyes, Mary Abrams was looking at me with more admiration than was comfortable.

"Okay, I'll go see Mrs. French."

"Goodie, and I'll go back to the newspapers and see what other things I can dig up on the vixen. Particularly her love life." Her face suddenly changed from happy and excited to frowning confusion. "Why would the thieves kill one of their own?"

"To keep him from talking. Perhaps the killer was high. After killing Brinkman, that person is now a security risk that could bring down the whole band. Thieves might not want to kill their victims, but when it comes to one of their own, self-preservation is a given."

"Oh, that reminds me." The dog got into her purse again and pulled out a white folded package. "I shouldn't have taken these, but I was pretty sure what they were."

"Why didn't you destroy them?"

She gave me a shrug and said, "Cops daughter."

CHAPTER 14

After Mary Abrams left, I opened the small package and stared at the three thick Russian cigarettes before lighting my own pipe. Were they really evidence, and of what? That Cedrick Brinkman liked to calm his nerves? Most of Hollywood was self-medicating, but whether it was prescribed or not depended on the price of the doctor.

I sniffed one of the things first and thought I smelled something more than just the strong odor of tobacco. Not being a drug dog, I couldn't pin down the sent. I pulled my penknife from my pocket and carefully slit one of the things lengthwise. The mouthpiece gave me some difficulty, but I managed to cut through that too. That's where I found the shiny segments of cardboard with printing on them.

Since I'd made a mess of the first one, I took a second cigarette and examined the mouthpiece before cutting. This time I managed not to shred the paper which turned out to be an engraved business card. Yulian Dalimil Psychic Consultant, by appointment only. A Stillwood Heights phone number was on the card but no address.

I didn't have to cut into the third cigarette but managed to tease the card out from inside the mouthpiece. It was the same card. Why would Brinkman hide a Psychic Consultant's business cards inside Russian cigarettes and store them in an embroidered case? If the hound knew a lot of lonely rich females, who knows what he was up to.

The two cigarettes I cut up I re-wrapped, but the third I wrapped up separately and locked both packages up in my desk. Only the card from the second cigarette lay on my desk as I smoked my pipe, debating on what to do.

The telephone rang, and I absently picked it up. Lieutenant Hartman was on the other end, and he wasn't happy. "Why did you lie about not knowing the female who gave you the ride?"

"Call me chivalrous, she did."

I thought I could hear the armadillo's teeth grind on the other end of the line before he broke the silence. "Mary Abrams' father was a good friend of mine. She came here and told me her side of the story."

"From what I hear, you told her a lot too."

"Mary is a curious dog. I told her a few things, yes, like I'm telling you now. We're handling the jewelry case, and you need to stay out of it. As for Brinkman's spare case, we tested the residue inside. Drugs."

"I wonder why he didn't smoke them?"

"Stay out of my case, Anoraq, or would you like to be locked up as a material witness?"

"Will I get three square meals a day?"

The male's answer was to hang up on me. Hartman was pushing hard for me to stay off the case. Why? I ended up pacing the floor of my office to calm down before coming back to the business card I'd found. Yulian Dalimil Psychic Consultant and con artist.

CHAPTER 15

The voice of the female who answered the telephone when I called was low, husky, and reminded me of a New Orleans street walker I'd seen in a movie once. She even had the mock creole accent down.

"I'd like to talk to Yulian Dalimil."

"Would you like to make an appointment? He is very busy."

"Today?"

"Next week. Perhaps the next. Let me check the book."

"Forget the book, lady, and write this down. The name's Lucius Anoraq." I rattled off my office address along with the telephone number. "Got it?"

"Yes, Mr. Anoraq."

"This is urgent. I want to see Dalimil about an Afghan hound by the name of Cedrick Brinkman."

"How very interesting. Perhaps you are with the police, no?"

The fake accent was annoying, but there was something else about the voice that put my fur on end.

"Are you listening? I'm a private detective, and the matter I'm wanting to see your boss about is life and death. Call me back with an appointment for today." I hung up the phone half hoping she wouldn't call back. Only she did ten minutes later.

"Mr. Dalimil will see you at six o'clock. We will send you a car." She hung up before I could object.

I checked my watch and decided I'd take dinner early.

Only I didn't make it to the elevator before I turned around and headed back to my office to use the telephone again. I knew a guy who worked for a title company on the Lot Books.

When I got him on the line I asked, "Can I get information about a property? I've got the address."

"Sure."

After I gave him the address to Mrs. Ginger Bloom's place, he said he'd call me back in fifteen minutes. It only took him ten. He gave me title lot and block number of the place and confirmed Mrs. Bloom was the owner. But come to find out, there were conditions to her ownership. The taxes and street bonds weren't that odd, but the first trust deed was.

"Isn't that one of those things where they can sell you out in minutes?" I asked.

"Not quite that fast, and the only thing odd is the amount. It's high for that neighborhood, two-thousand-six-hundred. Is the house new?"

"No, it's a broken-down old shack worth one-thousand-five-hundred at best."

"Something's off then. The place was refinanced a few years ago. Someone by the name of Cedrick Brinkman holds the deed. Does that help any?"

"Lots."

CHAPTER 16

This time when I arrived at Mrs. Blooms place, I didn't have any booze. Only before I got to the door, I saw the curtains twitch in the house next door and made a detour.

The front door of the neighbor's house could've been on a spring because it popped open as soon as I knocked, and a heron stuck her long neck out.

"Yes?"

"Hello, you wouldn't happen to be the female who called the police about Mrs. Bloom would you?"

Sharp eyes missed nothing as she looked me up and down. "And you are?"

"I'm a detective."

The bird's eyes lit up, and she bustled me into the house. "Land sakes, why didn't you say so. What's that old rat got up to now? I haven't seen or heard a thing since I called."

Unlike Bloom's place, the neighbor kept her house neat as a pin with doilies covering every surface.

"Haven't I seen you before? Yes, you're the one who visited her the other day before that hippo showed up."

"Speaking of the hippo, did the officers come here after they went to see Mrs. Bloom."

"Yes, but they didn't know a thing."

"Would you mind describing the hippo?"

"Certainly." The bird was good. She described Big Kelly in detail right down to the golf ball buttons. Evidently, he was driving a car too small for his large size, because the heron said he could barely fit into it. Too bad she didn't know a thing about cars.

"Do you know anything about Mrs. Bloom?"

"That rat isn't neighborly. Not one bit. She doesn't talk to anyone and plays that radio of hers all night. She doesn't even sing in tune." The heron leaned in close and stage whispered, "I think she drinks."

"Any visitors?"

"Not a one. Ten years she's been there. Even when she was married, and he wasn't much better than her. A drinker." She stuck her beak up close to my nose and asked, "Have you been drinking liquor?"

By the look in her eyes the old female thought alcohol was one of the seven deadly sins.

"Medicinal, I had a tooth pulled." It wasn't enough, she wasn't going to give me any more information, but I gave it a try. "Do you know if she was left with any money?"

"How would I know?"

"Does she live on relief?"

"This isn't that kind of neighborhood."

"I see, well you've been very helpful Mrs. I'm sorry, what was your name?"

"Mrs. Bitter."

"Well, thank you for your time."

I was halfway out the front door when she asked, "If I see anything, who should I call?"

"Detective Denson." I gave her the Doberman's number and figured he could use the information, if there was any.

"She get's a package at the first of the month, every month. Registered mail. Then after she gets it, she dresses up, goes out, and doesn't come back until late, liquored to the gills."

"Well Mrs. Bitter, I don't think she'll be getting anything registered mail tomorrow. It's April Fool's day."

The old bird's eyes gleamed with malicious intent and let out a laugh that sounded like a cross between a croak and a metal grinder.

CHAPTER 17

Nobody answered when I knocked on Mrs. Bloom's door, but the front screen door was unhooked and the main door open. Everything looked and smelled the same as last time as I walked through the door other than the radio was off and a second empty vodka bottle was on the floor next to the old one.

When I called out, I heard a noise from somewhere further into the house and sought it out. Mrs. Bloom was in her bedroom with the covers pulled up to her neck. The rat's bleary eyes cracked open to peek at me.

"Hello, Mrs. Bloom. Not feeling well?"

Her mouth moved slowly, and she licked the air as if it would wet her tongue before asking, "Did you get him?"

"If you're referring to Big Kelly, as far as I know, he's still on the loose. Are you scared of him?"

"Go away."

"Wouldn't you like to help us catch him?"

"Kelly's got money and friends, so you won't find him." Bloom licked the air again and asked, "Got any liquor?"

"Sorry, the wells dry. What happened to Big Kelly's female?"

"She died."

"How and where."

"I heard it was Texas. Pneumonia or something."

"Okay, here's a different question. Cedrick Brinkman holds the title on your house. Why is that?"

The rat stiffened. "I worked for him."

"Funny, after our last visit, he called me up and offered me a job. Thank you for giving him my card."

The odd noise that came out of her mouth didn't sound complimentary, but neither did the look of the banker's special she held when she pulled back the covers.

I backed up fast, out of the line of fire, but not before saying, "Think about working together, Mrs. Bloom." I made it out the front door without incident and headed off to see Denson.

When I got to the 77th Street Station and was told the Doberman was in, I started to wonder if the dog's rear was cemented to his chair. He looked gloomy as always, but this time he was picking his teeth when I walked into his office.

"Have you had any luck finding Big Kelly?" I asked and sat down.

"Nope, the hippo's gone. He's probably across the border by now. Are you still interested in finding him?"

"I'm more interested in the picture I left with you. The one of Jade Rose?"

"Oh yeah, the fox. Sure, I forgot about it, and the files already been turned in." Denson rifled through his desk and came up with the picture.

"So you won't mind if I keep it?"

"Go for it."

"Thanks."

After I put the thing in my pocket, Denson asked, "You still working on the case?"

"Not really. It's just a hunch."

"Let me know if it pans out."

"Sure thing," I said, and left the building to head back to my own office were the telephone was ringing.

"Hello, this is Lucius Anoraq, Private Detective."

"Mr. Anoraq, I'm calling for Mrs. Athena French. She requests your presence at the house as soon as convenient." The male on the other end gave me the address, and I told him I'd be ringing the doorbell shortly.

CHAPTER 18

Astor Drive was one of those places were nice houses followed the inland side and great mansions held the canyon side. A bat-eared fox wearing a blue Russian tunic and a permanent scowl stood in front of the half open gates of an estate.

Since I couldn't see a number anywhere, I stopped the car and asked, "Is this the French residence?"

The male took his time assessing me, my car, and my manner of dress before answering. "Yes, but nobody's in."

"Mrs. Athena Anne French called for me."

"Name?"

"Lucius Anoraq."

The male sauntered back to the gate house to use the telephone to call up to the house. After a discussion about my identity, he let me through. Two big Buicks sat in the driveway and made the small coupe parked next to them appear tiny, and the limousine dwarfed them all. The gardens were well tended but the mansion itself, though large, looked drab for southern California.

The butler met me at the door when I rang. He showed me through the house to a large sunny room with plenty of lounge chairs and a view of the Pacific Ocean. Two foxes and an Irish Setter mix sat around a table near the windows.

The Irish Setter mix I recognized as Mary Abrams. The male fox, looking old and moth eaten with the sharp suit he wore, I guessed to be Mr. French. Mrs. Athena French was obvious in the fact she looked like she just walked off the set of a big production.

"So good of you to come. Sweetie, get Mr. Anoraq a drink." The vixen never took her eyes off me as she gave her husband the order. Oddly enough, the old tod did as he was told and mixed a drink from the set up on the table in front of them.

After the old fox handed me my drink we sat down, and Mrs. French took control of the conversation. "Can you really help us, Mr. Anoraq? Without it being too much of a bother that is."

The vixen then crossed her legs in a careless manner and gave me a smile a person could feel in their back pocket.

"I doubt I could do much, considering there's not much to go on. If you don't mind my asking, how did Cedrick Brinkman manage to take you into his confidence?"

Mary Abrams was too innocent to take the hint of Mrs. French's sideways glance, but Mr. French must have been used to his wife's orders. "Isn't it time for your nap, sweetie?"

The fox nodded, got up, and left the room. While he was doing that Mrs. French downed her glass and fixed a new one. I got the impression the vixen could drink an elephant under the table.

"I take it that Mrs. Abrams here is in your complete confidence, Mr. Anoraq?"

"As far as she knows about the case."

The vixen's eyes narrowed, and she set her drink down. "You're too good looking of a male to be in this business. Is there much money in it?"

"No, not much money at all. But I like it, and it suits me. As for my looks, most people react the same way to Siberian Huskies. We're a pretty breed."

"You certainly are."

Mary Abrams finally got the hint and set down her mostly full glass. "If you'll excuse me, I think I have everything I need for my article. Don't worry, Mrs. French, I won't send it in without your approval."

The dog didn't look happy as she left and even looked back at us before closing the door.

"Isn't this better?" asked Mrs. French.

"You're probably wondering how that dog knows so much. She's a good detective in her own right though getting involved was by chance. The only reason she came around the night Brinkman was killed was she got suspicious."

Mrs. French grabbed her drink and took a swallow. "Poor Cedrick. He was a heel, but most of my friends are, but to die like that is tragic. Did he tell you about the hold up?"

"Not much. Seems you were coming back from Trocadero. Would you tell me your account of what happened? What I know of it seems… odd."

"Yes, it was, and I hardly ever wore the jade."

"Who knew you'd be wearing it that night?"

"My maid, but I trust her. She's had plenty of opportunity to steal from me, but she hasn't. The chauffeur was off that Thursday, so Cedrick drove. The coat I was wearing would have covered the necklace, so I doubt our butler or the footman would have seen it. Come to think of it, I don't remember even seeing the footman around."

"Who asked you to wear the necklace."

Instead of answering, she checked her watch.

"Whoever it is can wait," I said. "In this business, information is everything, so if you really want that bauble back, tell me what you remember of that night, in detail."

"Well then, why don't you come over here and sit by me, and we'll discuss it." She topped off my drink while I moved my rear.

If I wasn't careful, she might get me drunk and have her way with me. "I'd like to find your necklace, but I'd also like to find out who murdered Cedrick Brinkman. Call it a matter of principal. The dog paid me a hundred dollars, and I don't feel like I earned it. Tell me about that night. Your version please."

"Fine. After we left a party in Brentwood, Cedrick suggested we stop at Trocadero for a few drinks and dancing. Work was being done on Sunset, so he took Santa Monica. For some reason, I noticed the shabby little hotel we passed, maybe it was because of the single car parked in front of the beer joint across the street."

"Only one car?"

"Yes. The hotel was called Ibis Hotel, but I don't remember what the beer joint was called. The car followed us, and for some reason, Cedrick said he wanted to wander the roads and turned up a residential street. That's when the car following us drove ahead and cut us off. Once we were stopped, a male, at least he was dressed like a male, stepped out of the car and walked over to ours."

She took a sip of her drink and frowned. "He stayed out of the beam of the headlights and put a scarf over his face. In the darkness, I couldn't tell what species, but he was tall and thin. Once he got to the driver's side door, he held a gun and said, this is a stick up. The second male gave me a fright when he came out of nowhere and stood next to my door."

"You were distracted by the other guy and didn't see him sneak up."

"Yes. Well they asked for my jewelry and purse, so I handed them over. They then gave me back my purse and a ring and told me not to call the police or my insurance company about the jewels. That they would be contacting me with a ransom to get everything back. He wanted a nice smooth and easy deal and was willing to work with the insurance people but wanted to cut out a middleman. The one sounded educated while the other never spoke."

"Then what?" I asked.

"We headed home. I told Cedrick to keep his mouth shut, and I received a call the next day on my private phone, not the regular house phone."

"It's possible they bought the number from someone who has access to that kind of thing. Some Hollywood film stars have to change their numbers monthly."

"Well, I told the caller to deal with Cedrick and to be reasonable. They agreed and after some negotiation eight-thousand dollars was agreed on, and I handed the cash over to the hound."

"Do you think you could recognize the hold-up guys or the caller?"

"No," she said, and looked a little annoyed when saying it.

"Does Lieutenant Hartman know all this?"

"He does."

"Where did you meet Brinkman?"

"At the same radio station where I met my husband. Cedrick was an announcer. When he came into money, he left the station."

She downed another drink and was sure to top off mine. The vixen liked her booze, but I needed information more than drink. When I asked, "Do you know it for sure or is that something he said?" I got a shrug for an answer. "Did he borrow money from you?"

That question made her laugh. "If you're asking if Cedrick was a blackmailer the answer is yes. And a very high-class blackmailer at that. I got a little too drunk over at his house one night, and he took pictures."

"Bad dog."

"Very bad dog."

Two things happened at once, Mrs. Athena French planted one heck of a kiss on my lips, and Mr. French walked in on us. The old guy's polite cough and mumbled apology sobered me right up, while Athena French smiled in amusement.

I expected to get my ears chewed off and was surprised when the old fox shuffled back out the door. Athena French still had her arms around me, and I realized I had mine around her. I quickly disengaged myself from her arms and wiped my face with my handkerchief. Athena French looked unfazed.

"You do realize that your husband just walked in on us, right?"

"Oh, don't mind him. He knows he can't satisfy me in that way. But if it bothers you being in the house, then let's make it ten o'clock at the Belvedere Club. The place is owned by Mike Castle."

"Castle, isn't he good friends with the mayor of Bay City?"

She nodded.

I made my excuses and got out of there without being further molested.

CHAPTER 19

Mary Abrams was parked behind me sitting in her little coupe waiting for me. The Irish Setter didn't look too pleased, but she gave me a tight smile and asked, "What did you think of her?"

"That one could snap a mean garter."

The dog scowled and looked away. "Are all males gigolos?"

"Not all, but Brinkman certainly was, but then you already knew that."

"Excuse me?" The high yap and angry glare she gave me let me know I stuck my foot in it.

"I didn't mean from personal experience. You're a smart cookie."

"And you're a late comer to that party." The anger left her eyes and her ears twitched. "Do you want me to mind my own business? I just wanted to help."

"The thing is, I don't need help, the police don't want help, at least not from me, and I can't do a thing to help Mrs. French. The fox told some story about a beer joint where a car followed them from, but the jewel thieves are high-class. They had to be in order to know to nab the jade."

"Tipped off perhaps? Maybe by a psychic?" She gave me a sweet smile as her tail thumped on the car seat.

A cold chill creeped up my spine, and I wondered about the dog's lack of self-preservation. "Listen, Irish, there's a blanket over this case, big time. I've been warned off more than once. The French's have a lot of money they can pull strings with, and that's probably keeping a lid on everything. There's no news coverage, no random citizen to come forward with information, nothing. Something smells and not in a good way."

"You didn't get all the lipstick off." She started her car, pulled away from the sidewalk, and waved goodbye.

I stood there for a minute, watching the quiet neighborhood before slipping behind the driver's seat of my own car and wondered if I was sober enough to drive. I didn't think I'd drunk too much, but it was a little hard to measure when you weren't allowed to drain a glass.

Figuring I was okay, I headed back to the office. Mrs. French would be disappointed when I stood her up, but then again, I never agreed to meet her.

CHAPTER 20

The bear sitting in my waiting room reeked, and not in a way that makes you want to roll in the scent. His manner of dress was even worse. Everything he wore was two sizes too small. Only when he opened his mouth did I realized the part he was playing, and badly.

"You come now."

I walked by him, unlocked my office door, and walked in leaving the door open for him to follow.

"Who are you and where are we going?"

"Me, Berry-Berry. Great father say you come in iron chariot and—"

"Drop the act, please. You're hurting my ears." He was damaging more than my ears. It took effort not to bare my teeth and take a chunk out of his behind. Part of me wanted to drag him to the nearest reservation and see if the big idiot had a Jersey or Brooklyn accent. If there was one thing Hollywood was good at, it was proliferating blatant misconceptions.

The bear stopped talking, took his hat off, pulled a card out of the sweat band, and dropped it on my desk. It was the same business card as the ones hidden in the Russian cigarettes.

"What does your boss want?" I asked.

"He want—"

I let out a growl, and the bear had the sense to shut up.

"I usually get a hundred dollars as a retainer."

The bear looked me up and down and when he looked like he was going to speak again, I flattened my ears to my skull. Once he bought a clue, the bear took off his hat and again, fishing around the sweat band, pulled out a one-hundred-dollar bill, and tossed it on my desk.

I picked up the bill and put it in my pocket before pulling my gun and shoulder holster out of the desk drawer. The bear didn't flinch as I put it on.

"I've got my own car, I'll follow you," I said.

"No."

The stare down didn't last very long between us. The one thing about being alone is that standing up to big males can get you hurt and hurt bad. The ability to pick your battles was essential.

"Fine, we'll take your car."

CHAPTER 21

The dark blue Packard I got into was a seven-passenger custom made job that made me feel like I was in a high-end hearse. While I sat in the back, the bear sat up front next to the Ibis driving the thing.

The bird had a lead foot, but he knew how to handle the car. We drove up sunset, through Beverly Hills all the way to Stillwood Heights where the scent of sage had me sneezing. The road twisted an curved until it came to a long driveway in the middle of nowhere, with a modern monstrosity fit for a psychic to live in.

The car pulled up to the door, and the bear held the door for me to get out. He led me up a wide set of stairs to a black door which opened on its own accord. Nice theatrical stuff for the rich and impressionable.

Once inside the building, we took an elevator to another floor where the walls were heavily draped, and the lighting would have bordered on subterranean if not for the windows with a sea view.

A female Tapir sat behind a desk, but as soon as she opened her mouth, I knew it was the female who made the appointment for me. "Mr. Anoraq, so very good of you to come. Mr. Dalimil will be with you shortly."

I dropped the hundred-dollar bill on her desk and said, "Sorry, but I can't take this."

"Doesn't Mr. Dalimil wish to employ you?"

"I may not want the job. Haven't decided yet."

The Tapir slid the bill into her desk before getting up and conducting me into another room. This one was octagonal and reminded me of a tarot card reader's tent in a carnival.

The soft noise of a panel being moved beyond the curtains, caught my attention and a spiny bush viper emerged. His bright coloring only made his spiky scales look more exotic.

"Do sit down and be calm. Don't fidget or smoke, please. It breaks the spiritual flow. How can I be of service?"

I sat down, put a cigarette in my mouth but didn't light it. "That must wreak hell on your psychic waves because you've seemed to have forgot why I'm here. I gave the hundred-dollar bill back to your secretary. I'm here because of some Russian cigarettes laced with dope that had your card hidden away in the mouthpieces."

"Very strange. Unfortunately, there are things I do not know. This is one of them."

"Then what's with the carnival sideshow? As in the trained bear and the car ride."

"Berry-berry is a natural medium, very strong."

"And very smelly."

That got a hiss out of the viper. "You are a very stupid male, in a very stupid business."

"Yeah, whatever. What about your cards being in the cigarettes?"

"I have no power over what people do with my cards."

"Really, well these cards and cigarettes were in an embroidered case in the pocket of one Cedrick Brinkman."

The viper nodded. "Mr. Brinkman I know. I treated him for his camera shyness, but it didn't do any good. The camera didn't like him."

"Really? What if the dog wrote something in invisible ink on the back of your cards?"

The viper shrugged his thin shoulders and smiled.

"Then why have the bear hand over money," I asked.

"You are a professional, I unfortunately am considered a quack, that is all. Someone is always trying to, how you say, pull something."

The scent of the bear wafted up my nose, and I turned

to find the big guy sitting on a pillow, dressed in a white robe.

"Lovely, as if I didn't get a nose full of you on the drive here, I have to smell you again."

The bear didn't flinch, but the viper smiled and crossed his thin spiny arms. "Do get to the point Mr. Anoraq."

"Brinkman hired me to babysit him on an exchange. Money was involved. Only I got knocked in the head, and he was murdered. The dog had the cigarettes."

The news didn't cause a reaction in the viper. He was steady as a rock. He asked, "The police didn't find these cigarettes, did they? That's why you are here?"

A flicker of a smile passed his lips as he asked another question. "Do you have them?"

"One, and not on me. While the things don't prove much, they seemed an odd thing to carry." When the viper didn't stop me or ask questions, I asked, "Do you know Mrs. Athena Anne French? The vixen is loaded and lives in Bay City."

"I treated her for a slight impediment of speech."

"Everybody knows everybody in this case. She knew Brinkman."

"If you're here to blackmail me, it won't work. I have plenty of friends to deal with those type of people."

I could have tried to stare him down, but that would have been pointless considering the guy had no eyelids. The viper leaned forward on the table to caress a crystal ball.

"Brinkman was the blackmailer. The Afghan hound blackmailed a lot of females along with helping out a pack of jewel thieves. I wonder who told him which to cultivate in the first place?"

"And you think it was me?"

"You're in the racket. Dress it up any way you like with crystals and cards, it's still a racket."

The viper didn't move, but the lights went out.

CHAPTER 22

I got up in a hurry, kicking back the stool I was sitting on and drawing my gun. Too bad my coat was buttoned, slowing me down. But it wouldn't have mattered. The big bear was on me in a heartbeat. Whether it was a sap or his fist at the back of my head, it didn't matter, I was seeing stars. The hit wasn't enough to knock me out, but it did make me easier to disarm. I would have rather been knocked out because the bear started choking the life out of me.

Nothing I did loosened the bears grip. Beating or clawing at his arms with my fist didn't do a thing, and it wasn't like I could bite him. I started to see stars again in the darkness, and my blood pounded in my ears.

"Let him breathe," said Dalimil as the lights of the room came back on. "Sit him up."

The respite wasn't much as I felt someone search my pockets. I knew they'd find what they were looking for.

"Only one cigarette? Where are the others?"

The bear was good. He understood how to inflict pain without the person passing out.

"At the office, two more."

"You're probably lying, but no matter, I can find out," said the viper.

This time, when the bear choked me, I managed to get hold of one of his fingers and twisted. I ended up with another hit to the head for my troubles, but at least he let me go. Dalimil scaly face floated in front of me, and he smiled. I swung a fist at that smile and connected.

He hissed, and I saw his fangs, but he stopped just shy of striking. "Fool." The viper touched his face as a trickle of blood seeped from his nose. "I can use this to my advantage. I have guests coming to deal with you."

I'm not sure if I passed out, or if they knocked me out, all I knew is I stopped hurting for a while.

CHAPTER 23

The hand that hauled me to my feet was attached to a bobcat. "Come on mutt, let's get you moving."

My feet didn't want to walk straight, and my brain felt fuzzy as the guy pushed me into the reception room with all the windows. It was dark out now.

"Sit." The bobcat pushed me into a chair. I didn't want to sit but at least I could look around. A Greater sage grouse was talking to the Tapir. It looked like she was reading the bird something from a notepad. Dalimil was standing by the windows, looking out into the darkness, but the bear was nowhere to be seen.

Dalimil half turned and smiled at me. His nose didn't look so pretty anymore.

"So, you out here having fun, mutt?" The bobcat was talking, but he wasn't saying much. The male was looking at my wallet. "What's a peeper from the big city doing out here? A bit a blackmail?"

My throat hurt from being choked, and I figured I had a few bruises.

Having finished with the Tapir, the grouse walked up beside the bobcat and straightened his tie.

I managed to croak out a word. "Cops?"

The bobcat showed his fangs. "Smart mutt."

The grouse didn't say a word, but by the glazing over one eye, I knew he wasn't a Los Angeles cop. The bird would have been retired if that was the case.

When the bobcat handed me back my wallet, I was surprised to find nothing missing. "Give me back my gun," I said.

"The mutt wants his gun back." The bobcat looked sideways at the grouse and smiled. "And what you going to do with it, mutt?"

"Thought I'd shoot a bear."

"Shoot a bear? Aren't you a tough guy?"

"Are you going to repeat everything I say, Hemingway?"

That confused the bobcat. "My name's not Hemingway. Is this guy crazy?"

"Perhaps, a little unbalanced," said Dalimil. The viper didn't move from his place at the windows.

While the bobcat complained about me calling him Hemingway, the grouse finally spoke up. "What's this about a gun?"

"It's inside, I'll get it." The viper slithered past, and the grouse followed. When they came back, the grouse handed me my hat and my gun, minus the bullets of course.

"Okay, let's go." The bobcat kept a hand on my arm all the way to the elevator.

CHAPTER 24

The plain sedan they bundled me into had private plates. I sat up front with the bobcat, and the grouse got in the back. The bobcat ran his mouth, while the grouse kept quiet, other than to say, "Hurry up." We drove down the curving roads away from Yulian Dalimil.

"Say, how come you don't have a car, mutt?" asked the bobcat.

"Because the viper wanted to see me."

That made the feline laugh. "Mr. Dalimil said you called him up with a story, so he wanted to figure out who you was and what you was up to first."

"Plus, he knew he'd be calling you two, and I wouldn't be needing a car."

"Well, he had a Dictaphone under his table, and that secretary of his typed everything up and read off what was said to Mr. Renton here."

"Doubt that. They probably have a bunch of stock notes for every occasion."

"Then why don't you tell us what you went to see him for, mutt?"

"Before you cave my skull in? Will you bury me in a shallow grave?"

"We don't work like that."

"You know Dalimil very well."

"I just take orders. Mr. Renton knows him. He knows everybody and everybody knows him."

Exhaustion creeped into my bones as we drove through the darkness, and I almost nodded off when the bobcat asked, "Why you call me Hemingway?"

"Because he was another person who repeats himself." I was beginning to wish I'd kept my mouth shut. The feline didn't have enough brain cells to get the gag.

The bobcat drove down a dirt road that ran along the back of a mountain. After a mile or so the bird said, "Stop."

We stopped, and the bobcat turned to face me. "Nice knowing you. Now be on your way and don't come back."

"Out here in the middle of nowhere? Well, at least it'll give me time to figure out why a couple of Bay City cops are working outside their jurisdiction."

"That'll be hard to prove, mutt."

"So long, Hemingway." I had my foot on the running board when I sensed movement. The next thing I knew was darkness.

CHAPTER 25

Smoke filled the room. It hung in the air swirling in slow lethargic waves. Nothing looked familiar, and there were bars across the windows.

I managed to yell, "Fire," and a white coated pelican stormed into the room with a sap in his hand.

With a yawn, I turned over. "Nightmare. Where am I?"

"Where you belong. Do I need to put you back in the straight-jacket or you going to be quiet?"

"I'm going to sleep."

"You do that." The pelican left the room, and I heard the jangle of keys as the door locked.

The pelican hadn't disturbed the smoke, it still hung in the air. When I looked down at myself, I wore flannel hospital pajamas. I tried touching my face, but my hands were numb, and it was an effort to move my limbs. Thinking wasn't easy, but I knew it was nighttime because of the darkness outside the windows.

When I looked up at the glass domed light attached to the ceiling, little faces peered back at me and asked nonsense questions. I felt like I was in a Lewis Carroll book.

Whatever was wrong with me, I knew I had to fight it and managed to sit up on the bed. That's when I noticed the straps attached to the side. Somehow, I knew they were the reason my hands were numb. A bottle of whisky sat on the side of the sink, and I managed to stagger over and take a drink. The stuff was tainted, and I barely made it to the washbowl in time to toss my guts up.

Someone was having a laugh at my expense. When the nausea passed, I made it back to the bed to rest a bit and realized my arm was sore. Checking beneath the fur I found bruising. With it came the realization that I'd been doped. With what, I had no idea, but I needed to get it out of my system.

What could I do but walk and drink water from the tap in the corner of the room? The water made me feel better, but the walking wasn't easy. I had to push myself. I pushed myself until I was ready to talk to someone.

CHAPTER 26

The door was locked, and the single chair bolted to the floor, so I stripped the bed down to the springs and ten minutes later I managed to pull one of the metal pieces free. Then I remembered the whisky bottle. It would have worked the same and not bruised my knuckles. I grabbed the bottle and dropped the spring.

After a rest and a drink of water, I shuffled over to the door and planted my back to the wall. I took several deep breaths before letting out the loudest howl I could manage. I kept howling as I heard the key in the lock and watched the pelican pop through the door, ready to use his sap. The mess I made of the bed brought him up short and gave me time to use the bottle on his head.

The bird had a hard head and didn't go down without a fight, and both of us got a few bruises. When the bird was out, I checked his breathing then put the bed back together. The straps came in handy for restraining the male. With not only his sap, but his keys in hand, I was able to unlock the closet and find my clothes. My gun was in its holster, but my money was gone. When I checked the pelican's wallet, I found where it had wandered off to.

Getting dressed was doable, though I had to stop and rest. Once I had myself together, I left the room and locked the door. The place was silent.

Thick carpeting covered the hallway, muffling my footsteps. No sound came from the three other closed doors, and only the odor of antiseptic reached my nose. The house was old and probably sat on some quiet residential street somewhere. Stained glass windows lay at the end of the hall. A door, this one cracked open with light streaming through, was just past the stairs leading to the floors below.

Curiosity had me moving closer. The rustling of paper and the squeak of springs had me pausing, but when nothing happened, I moved closer and peered carefully into the room.

Unlike the white cell I was kept in, this room looked more like a hotel room with colors and comfort in mind. The hippo inside sat on the bed reading the newspaper and chain smoking judging by the mounting cigarette stubs that filled the ashtray beside the bed. I'd found Big Kelly.

With having dealt with the hippo once, I had no intention of dealing with him again and hurried down the stairs as fast as I dared go.

When I reached the bottom, I found another partially open door and heard the murmurings of a conversation. After a dry clicking sound of the handset of a telephone being dropped in its carriage, the murmuring stopped.

I waited and listened before walking through the door.

CHAPTER 27

The office was small, neat, and professional. The mouse that sat at the desk also looked the part with his large spectacles and white coat. He looked at me with disapproval, but his hand was close to the corner of his desk.

I held up the sap. "Don't bother with the buzzer, doc, the bird's tied up."

"You are a very sick male, sir. You shouldn't be up and about."

I responded by sapping his right hand before it could reach the gun hidden inside the drawer. The mouse recoiled to nurse his fingers while I pulled out the gun. It carried the same load as mine, so I switched the magazines.

When the mouse moved, I pointed the gun at him. "If you have another buzzer that's wired to the police chief, I don't suggest you using it."

"There isn't any."

"Got any whisky?"

The mouse nodded and pulled out a bottle. Not wanting a repeat of dealing with a tainted bottle, I made sure he took the first sip.

"So, doc, tell me if I'm wrong, but was I drugged or at least knocked out, and brought here to be tied to a bed with no food or water? Why all the trouble for someone who's unimportant?"

When the mouse didn't say anything I added, "I may not have been drugged up before I got here, but I certainly was after."

I dropped the sap on his desk. "The staff here are very persuasive."

"Do hand over the gun please, Mr. Anoraq. You've been a very sick male, and I must insist you go back to bed."

"And you are? What time and day is it?

"To answer your first question, I'm Dr. Winkler. It is now midnight Sunday. You were brought in Friday night suffering from narcotic poisoning, and I gave you digitalis three times to keep you alive. When you screamed and fought us, you had to be restrained."

"You're no doctor. Not a real one. A body doesn't move from narcotics poisoning because they're in a coma. Who put me in this place?"

"A couple of Bay City Police officers brought you here. A Sergeant Petoskey, I believe. He said he found you wandering around in a daze and thought you'd overdosed."

"Nice story. Why keep me here?"

"You were sick."

"Well, I'm not now, so I'm leaving."

The mouse's whiskers twitched. "But you can't, you'll be arrested immediately."

"Really? Would you like to try opening that safe that's behind you? It looks awful big. Too big for a medical facility."

"Absolutely not." The mouse's whiskers twitched even worse now.

"Interesting, I'm the one holding the gun. People usually do what their told when a gun is involved. Bye, doc." I backed out the door, and when I was out of view, hurried for the front door. It was unlocked. Fear was probably the only thing that kept me on my feet as I checked the addresses and street signs for a location. All the while, I listened for the sounds of police sirens as I walked the streets.

Several blocks over, I found Mary Abrams' street. Double checking the addresses, I followed the numbers until I came across her small brick house surrounded by rosebushes. A light was still on in the house.

The adrenaline had burned off along with the whisky, and I staggered up the walkway to ring the bell.

A small peephole slid open in the door and a wet nose appeared, sniffing the air. "Who is it?"

"Anoraq."

The dog opened the door wide, and I nearly fell inside.

CHAPTER 28

The living room was nice and comfortable without puffery or frills. I lounged in an overstuffed chair, having eaten toast with eggs and working on my fourth cup of coffee, this one laced with bourbon.

Mary Abrams sat across from me looking worried. I'd told her almost everything of what happened, leaving things like Big Kelly out of the conversation.

"I thought you were drunk," she said. "All I could think about was you running around with that vixen. I thought… oh, I don't know what I thought."

"Jealous?"

"Maybe."

"She didn't strike me as your type."

A well thrown pillow bounced off my head, and I almost spilt my coffee.

"You've got a nice place here," I said. "Did the writing get it or something else?"

"Writing didn't get me anything. The house is my inheritance. Dad wasn't on the take, but he did have some plots in Del Ray that turned out to have oil on them." She stared at me for a while before saying, "I'm glad you took a closer look at those Russian cigarettes."

"Unfortunately, the cards hidden in them didn't go anywhere."

"What are you talking about? You got beat up and stuck in a liquor cure house over the weekend. That psychic is in with a high-class mob, or perhaps leads it."

"No, it's more complicated than that."

"Do tell." Mary rested her head on her hand and glared at me.

"Yulian Dalimil may be a ruthless viper, but I can't see him as the brains of an entire outfit. At least, not the jewelry angle. If he was, I doubt if I would have gotten out of that dope hospital alive. Not to mention, he didn't get pissy until I mentioned Brinkman might have used invisible ink on those cards. Something I threw out there to see if I could get a rise out of the reptile."

"So there isn't any writing on the cards?"

I shrugged in answer. "Brinkman was afraid of something and probably figured anything found on his body would end up in police custody. If Dalimil is a crook, why were the cigarettes left on the dog's body to be found?"

"Do you mean that Dalimil isn't connected to Brinkman's murder?"

"That's exactly what I'm thinking."

The Irish Setter shifted in her chair, and her floppy ears moved forward. "Isn't the viper connected with the jewel thieves?"

"I'm beginning to think that was an assumption on our part. A wrong assumption."

We sat in silence for a while before she said, "You must be tired."

"A bit. Would you mind driving me to a taxi stand?"

"After everything you've been through?" she asked. "You could stay here, you know. Bed or couch, your choice."

"I kind of want to be in my own place. Besides, you live here in Bay City. If any of the bad guys connect you to me, things might get difficult for you."

"Bay City isn't that bad. It's a nice town."

"So is Chicago, unless you come across mobsters with tommy guns. Taxi, please."

The female let out a low growl, then got up and grabbed her coat, hat, and purse. "Has anyone told you that you're a royal pain."

"Several and frequently."

Mary Abrams did more than drive me to a taxi stand, she drove me all the way back to my apartment. We parted with me reminding her to lock her doors.

It was well past eleven, so I had to use my keys to get through the lobby doors. The building was quiet, and milk bottles sat in front of service doors. Once inside my own apartment, I stood in the darkness for a few minutes, inhaling the scent of home.

After crawling into bed, the only thing that woke me were the nightmares, but those were few.

CHAPTER 29

I stared at the ceiling while I debated the reasons, both pro and con, for getting out of bed. Someone knocking on my apartment door tipped the scales, and I heaved myself from the mattress only to stub my toe on the way to the door.

Lieutenant Hartman was on the other side and didn't look happy. The armadillo could have rolled himself up into a ball and used me as a bowling pin, but instead he pushed inside and shut the door.

"I've been looking for you." The male's focus wasn't on me but on my apartment. "Where have you been? You certainly haven't been here."

"Trust me, I wish I had been."

"Knock off being a smart ass."

"I'll need coffee for that. Would you like to join me?"

I grabbed a pack of cigarettes off the end table and lit up while the armadillo scowled at me. "I warned you to stay out of this on Thursday."

"Wasn't that Friday?"

"Thursday, Friday, it doesn't matter. Do you realize how much trouble I can make for you? Do you have any idea why I haven't?"

"Don't tell me it's my sparkling personality." I batted my eyelashes at him and headed into the kitchen.

Hartman followed me, but his lemon sucking expression didn't change as he lit his own cigarette and puffed away. The male was nice enough to put his burnt match in the ashtray rather than on the floor.

"Warning you off seemed like a good thing at the time, but I didn't know you were withholding evidence."

"Evidence?"

That got me another cold glare, but I ignored it by concentrating on the coffee. The armadillo was still scowling when I pulled two cups out of the cupboard and placed them on the kitchen table.

"If you're not careful, your face is going to freeze like that," I said. It was his turn to ignore me. "What's so wrong with me seeing Athena French if she sends for me?"

"Forcing your way into her place and insinuating a scandal doesn't qualify for being sent for."

I added another scoop of grounds after hearing that. "That's not the way I remember it. We hardly talked about the job at all. There certainly wasn't much to her story or any leads."

"The beer joint in Santa Monica is a known crook's hangout, and the hotel across the street is just as bad."

"Did she say I forced myself on her as well?" I asked and watched the armadillo blush. Something I thought impossible.

"No, she didn't."

"Good, because I was lucky to get out of there with my virtue intact. The liquor that vixen serves is top shelf, and she doesn't like empty glasses."

With the coffee done, I poured two mugs and set the second in front of him. He took a sip and some of the grouchiness left his countenance.

"The jewel thieves have been working the Hollywood area for the last ten years," he said. "They went too far when they killed Brinkman."

"At least we agree on something."

"Well, I'm hoping to break it. Really break it and not just have a token arrest."

"You're one of the good guys?"

"I try to be."

We drank in silence, and I refilled our cups to make another pot.

"Where were you?" asked Hartman.

"In Bay City. When I ran into a bit of trouble with the cops, or at least two guys pretending to be cops, they took me to a private hospital instead of the jail cell. I'm lucky to have gotten out."

"Damn right you are. Bay City is not a place you want to play around."

"It was a rough weekend. I've been sapped, beaten, choked, doped, tied up, and lord only knows what else while I was off my head, but I made it home. Unfortunately, I can't prove one incident. It's all hearsay. Other than the bruises and needle marks, and they're not worth shaving for."

Most of the anger had left his face, and the male looked at me in wonder. "Why were you in Bay City?"

"The cops took me there; I was actually in Stillwood Heights, which is Los Angeles. I went to see a psychic about some cigarettes. Have you ever heard of Yulian Dalimil? Three Russian cigarettes had his cards hidden in the mouthpieces, and I couldn't figure out why Brinkman had them if he never intended to smoke them."

"Why didn't you tell me? Mary already told me she'd swiped them."

"She should be careful. One of these days, she's going to get herself into trouble that you can't get her out of."

Hartman eyeballed me and said, "You could always take over that job. She likes you."

"No, I can't. Mary's a nice female, but not my type."

"What's the matter? Is it a breed thing?"

"No, but I did fail my breeding exam."

The armadillo looked at me in confusion but didn't ask for enlightenment.

"Getting back to Brinkman's murder," I said. "And you've probably figured this out already, but let me give you my theory. Brinkman liked blackmailing females.

Athena French confirmed as much. The dog also dealt with the jewel robbers by cultivating victims and setting the stage for the heists. The heist of the jade necklace was obviously a setup, if Brinkman hadn't altered his usual route, it never would have happened."

"If the chauffeur was driving, it wouldn't have changed much," said Hartman. "But too many heists with Brinkman would have rumors flying."

"With that kind of racket, you don't want rumors. Plus, the stuff was sold back cheap. Somebody talked which meant Brinkman became a liability."

"Hence the reason he was bumped off."

I got up to grab the coffeepot and refilled our cups. "People don't retire or leave those rackets. Brinkman probably suspected something was wrong, and that's why he asked me along for the ride. Only he didn't confide in me, so I walked in blind. The one thing he did do was have something on him that would point to someone in the organization who was ruthless. The cigarettes were something a pup might think up, but it worked."

"Professionals wouldn't leave a body, not unless they wanted the hit to look like an amateur job. That way they can get a new guy and stay in business."

"Exactly."

Hartman scratched an ear. "Why Dalimil? I've already checked the viper out, and with the racket he's already running, why bother with the jewel heists?"

"Because what he does may not always be in fashion. And some people can never have enough money."

"I'll take another look at him then. What about Brinkman? The dog had one of your cards."

"I forgot about that." This time it was me scratching behind my ears.

"The dog had twenty-three thousand dollars hidden in a safe deposit box, along with bonds and a trust deed on some property. The address was interesting. If I hadn't been behind with reading homicide and doubtful death reports, I would have spotted the connection earlier."

"Big Kelly?" When Hartman nodded at my question, I said, "Lieutenant Denson has that case."

"A sloth on sedatives would have a better chance of solving the case."

"Tell me how you really feel."

The scowl briefly returned to Hartman's face. "Denson told me everything about the case. It turns out that the property Brinkman has the trust deed on used to be where this Jade Rose female used to live." The armadillo didn't have to rattle off the address for me to know it, though he did anyway.

"One second." I got up from the table to find my coat and the pictures in the pocket. For a brief moment, I worried that I'd lost them, but they were there, and I brought them back to the kitchen to show Hartman. "That's Big Kelly's female. Only she's supposed to be dead according to Mrs. Bloom, the current resident of the house. This one is of Mrs. Athena Anne French."

The armadillo's eyes lingered on the photo of Jade Rose. "Nice legs."

"What would you do if I told you that the hospital I was being held at in Bay City, was run by a mouse called Dr. Winkler? And that he was running a crook's hideout? Big Kelly was there the same time I was. Only his room was a lot nicer."

"Are you sure?"

"Once you see Big Kelly in person, you can't unsee him."

"I want to see this Bloom female, but... Describe Dr. Winkler." I did, and he asked to use my telephone. Whoever he contacted, it was a long conversation. When he came back to the kitchen, I had boiled eggs, made toast, and was about to sit down and eat.

"A state narcotics guy is going to check out Dr. Winkler and his private hospital using a fake complaint to nose around. He won't get Big Kelly, that male would have been moved right after you left, but he might find something else."

"You don't trust the Bay City cops?"

The look on the armadillo's face said it all. "We'll pick up those Russian cigarettes from your office on the way. Finish eating and let's go."

"Can I get dressed first? I don't want to get arrested and sent back to the hospital for running around in my pajamas."

"There's a thought."

I cocked my head to the side and asked, "Is Bay City that corrupt?"

"Mike Castle may be rich, but he's nothing but a two-bit crook. He paid thirty grand to have his candidate elected into the position. He doesn't just own several clubs but the two gambling ships off the coast."

We used Hartman's car to get to my office. Not only did I have mail, but the cigarettes were where I'd left them, and there was no sign of the office being searched.

Hartman sniffed the cigarettes before pocketing them. "There must not have been anything on the cards. Dalimil must have figured you were trying to put something over on him."

CHAPTER 30

The heron poked her beak out the front door, and I could tell she recognized me.

"Hello, Mrs. Bitter. This is Lieutenant Hartman from headquarters. Can we have a word? It won't take long."

"Of course." The bird stepped back and waved us in before shutting the door.

"Did she get it?" I asked.

A wicked smile crossed the heron's face. "No, she didn't. She even ran after the mailman, when he didn't come up her walk yesterday. When he told her that he didn't have anything, she had a fit and slammed the door to her house."

Hartman looked out the window at the side of Mrs. Bloom's house. Mrs. Bitter turned on him suddenly and asked, "Do you have a badge?"

He dug in his pocket and came up with the gold and blue enameled shield to show her.

The bird nodded, "Nothing happened on Sunday of course, other than she went out for a couple of bottles of alcohol."

"When the mailman passes her up again today, she's really going to get sore."

She nodded in agreement. "There were folks there last night. I only saw them leaving on account I went to the pictures. But when I got home, a car left out of there with no lights on. I couldn't get the license number."

I pointed out the window at the blue uniformed yak with a heavy leather bag. "You're slipping. Though we did distract you."

The herons head swiveled, and her mouth dropped open. "Land sakes. Where is she? I would have thought she'd have chased him down." A few seconds later, we heard the sound of mail being pushed through her mailbox.

"How often do you have the mail delivered in this neighborhood, Mrs. Bitter?" asked Hartman.

"Twice. There's the morning post and the afternoon. Though come to think of it, registered mail is special delivery."

"You said Mrs. Bloom ran after the regular mailman, but nothing about special delivery."

Mrs. Bitter twisted the apron she was wearing in her feathered hands and looked away. "I must have been mistaken."

"I see." Hartman eyeballed her a bit before letting her off the hook. "We'll be going now, Mrs. Bitter. Thank you for your time."

We let ourselves out and headed over to the Blooms residence. The washing still hung on the line in the side yard, but no one answered the door when we knocked or rang the bell.

"Try the door, she had it unlocked last time," I said.

The door was locked. Hartman looked up and down the street before asking, "Back door?"

"Let's check." We walked around the back of the house only to have the screen door secured with a hook. Hartman pulled out his pocketknife and slipped the larger blade between the screen door and the jamb, lifting the hook. We walked straight up the steps onto the porch.

"Do you think the bird will call the cops on us?" I asked.

"Don't know, don't care. How can anyone live like this?" Flies buzzed by us as we maneuvered past the junk and empty bottles only to find the back door locked as well.

"This isn't right. The rat is too sloppy to do this. Something's wrong."

"Shall we?"

"We shall." I elbowed the glass in the door and used my hat to remove the shards before I reached in to unlock the door. More flies met us in the kitchen.

The radio was off in the living room, and Hartman pointed at it. "Nice and expensive. It's also unplugged."

"I bet the volumes up, but what concerns me is the smell."

"Everything smells in here."

"But I smell blood."

We made a bee line to Mrs. Bloom's bedroom, only to find her laying on her bed with her head smashed in.

"Looks like poor old Denson will have to do some work."

CHAPTER 31

A big black bug kept me amused while I sat opposite Hartman's desk and listened to the activities of the room. Another detective talked in hushed tones on the telephone, and the dull voice over the police loudspeaker box rattled off the latest incident with a description of the perpetrator.

Hartman bustled back into the room, holding a sheaf of papers, his armored body zipping around desks and people like a dancer rather than the mini tank he was born to be. He dropped the papers in front of me and sat in his chair. "There's four copies, sign them all."

"Your lunch is getting away," I said and grabbed a pen.

"That's not mine. It's still wiggling. And don't try to distract me. Will you please leave this case alone?"

Instead of answering, I signed the paperwork and stared at him with my ears forward.

"No prints were found at the Bloom's residence. The rat probably turned the radio up herself, but someone else probably pulled the plug. We didn't find anything on it or the cord. Why they bothered to mess with the thing is anyone's guess. She wasn't shot; her neck was broken. Her head was caved in after she was dead."

I lit a cigarette and let the armadillo talk.

"This guy, Big Kelly, he could have been sore at her. The reward money for turning him in all those years ago was paid to a guy now dead, but Mrs. Bloom could have gotten a cut, and the hippo found out. While we might be able to tie Big Kelly to the murder by the spacing of the bruises on the rat's neck, none of the neighbors saw much of anything that night."

"Big Kelly didn't intend to kill her. The male doesn't know his own strength."

"He still killed her." Hartman heaved a sigh. "Why don't you go home, get some rest, and let us handle finding Big Kelly and deal with Brinkman's murder."

"Brinkman paid me to keep him safe, and I failed. Now, Athena French has hired me. It's not like I can retire and laze around at the beach for the rest of my days."

"Any captain could make you regret digging."

"Not with the French's on my side."

The male nodded. "Perhaps, but you could still find yourself in a bind if you're not careful."

"That's the story of my life."

Hartman tapped his long nails on the desk. "Dalimil is out of town but the wife and secretary aren't saying where. As for the bear, he's disappeared too."

"If you're going to ask me to sign a complaint, we both know it won't stick, so why bother."

This time he nodded and sighed. "The wife has never heard of you, and the Bay City cops are not my jurisdiction. I'd say it was a good guess that those cards and cigarettes were a plant to have us running in the wrong direction."

"What about Dr. Winkler?"

"The whole operation must have lit out of there as soon as you left. The house is empty though there are lots of prints. Winkler probably has a record somewhere for something. The case will be handed over to the Feds. If he's got protection from one of the rackets, it'll depend on how much flack they're willing to take to keep him in business."

"What do you know about Mike Castle?"

"A rich gambler." Hartman shook his head. "I can't see him getting involved with something that could tie back to him. Not Brinkman's murder. By the way, there were some letters in the dog's safe deposit box. It seems Mrs. Bloom used to work for Brinkman."

"How convenient."

"I know it doesn't make sense, but what if Brinkman was a superstitious dog and Mrs. Bloom was his good luck piece?"

"That makes me wonder who's good luck piece Brinkman was." I said.

"Not yours." His voice was full of steel, and while I got the message, we both knew I wasn't going to take his advice.

CHAPTER 32

The drive down to Bay City was uneventful, but the City Hall building was a surprise. I would have expected something more austere rather than cheap. Several bums sat on the retaining wall outside the three-story building, but it was the well fed clump of City Hall fixers milling outside the double doors who were being nuisances. I finally managed to squeeze past a giraffe and penguin, and both gave me dirty looks like I hadn't said, "excuse me," multiple times already.

The steps outside the building were cracked, and whoever was paid to keep the inside clean was falling down on the job. With a little more sunlight, weeds could grow between the tiles. A small wooden sign pointed the way to the police information desk where a uniformed mutt snoozed, oblivious of his surroundings.

I managed to find the Chief's office on the second floor behind a door marked Edgar Ward, Chief of Police. Enter. The muskox on secretarial duty looked at my card, yawned, and moved his bulk off his chair to lumber through another mahogany door marked, Edgar Ward, Police Chief, Private.

When the muskox returned, he held the door open for me. The room was large, cool, and had a nice view out the windows that covered three walls. The Aye-aye that sat at the desk looked me over with his big-eyed stare while he popped termites from a candy dish into his mouth using his long middle finger.

Someone once told me that Aye-ayes were related to

lemurs, but if you asked me, they look more like wingless, long tailed bats, off a month long drunk and strung out on dope.

"Sit down, Mr. Anoraq, and tell me what I can do for you."

"I was hoping you'd be able to straighten out a few things for me."

"If it's a parking ticket, I'm afraid you'll have to pay it."

"This is a little more serious than parking tickets. Do you have a sergeant, a bobcat, working for you by the name of Petoskey? Or for that matter a Greater sage grouse by the name of Renton."

"Yes, I believe so. As for Captain Renton, he's the chief of Detectives."

"Mind if I talk to them in your office?"

The Aye-aye stopped munching, picked up my card that was sitting in front of him, and looked it over. "Why would you want to do that?"

"Do you know a psychic named Yulian Dalimil? The viper lives in Stillwood Heights at the top of the hill."

"Stillwood Heights is outside our jurisdiction."

"That's what I thought. Only when I went to see Mr. Dalimil regarding a client of mine, the viper got the crazy idea I was there to blackmail him. Guess a guy can get paranoid in that type of business. The bear he had as a bodyguard struck first and didn't bother with questions. The next thing I knew, he called Petoskey and Renton to take me off his hands. They drove me some distance away and left me unconscious."

Edgar Ward stared at me for some time before asking, "And this was in Stillwood Heights?"

"Yes, but you probably think I'm making the whole thing up."

"Then you won't mind finding your own way out?" When I didn't move his hand moved toward what I assumed was a hidden buzzer.

"Please don't make the same mistake they did, Chief.

I'm not here to file a complaint because anyone fool enough to do what they did would cover their tracks. I'd like to correct the misunderstanding and thought perhaps Sergeant Petoskey would be willing to give me a hand. Not only would it make my job easier, but my employer would appreciate any assistance the Bay City police force could give."

His eyes narrowed. "And who would your employer be?"

"Mrs. Athena Anne French."

I didn't think the guy could look any more tripped out, but I think his eyelids disappeared into his head.

"Lock the door, please."

I did so, and when I came back to my seat, a bottle of vodka and two glasses were on the desk. Ward had a dopy smile on his face while he poured and said, "The job you're doing for Mrs. French, does it have anything to do with Mr. Dalimil?"

"A connection, but you can call her and confirm I'm telling the truth."

"Good idea." Ward looked through what he called his little black book of campaign contributors, picked up the telephone, and dialed. It took time to get past the person who answered and get Mrs. French on the line, but when he did, from the face he made, he wished he didn't. The guy finally handed me the handset. "She wants to talk to you."

With a smirk, I took the handset, "This is Lucius.

"What are you doing with that ridiculous male?" she asked.

"At the moment, drinking vodka, but I'm hoping to clear up some business. Has anything new happened on your end?"

"No, other than you stood me up."

I let my voice drop to a silky tone. "I'm sorry about that, but I ran into some trouble. Let me make it up to you."

"Tonight?"

"How about I call you to make sure I don't run into trouble again?"

"Are you playing hard to get? Don't tell me I'm playing the fool."

"You are. I'm a poor dog who likes to pay his own way. And it's not as soft as you might like."

"All you males are alike." She hung up before I could make any snappy comebacks.

The chief continued staring at me, only this time his mouth was open.

"Her husband doesn't care," I said and filled both glasses.

After downing his, the chief put the bottle away. "I see, well, I'll have Sergeant Petoskey come up if he's around."

While I unlocked the door, Ward flipped a switch on his call box and told his secretary to find the bobcat. The wait didn't take long. The male didn't even look at me when he walked through the door but focused on Ward. Though we didn't need to be introduced, the chief did it anyway.

"Sergeant, this is Mr. Lucius Anoraq, he's a private detective from Los Angeles. He has a rather interesting story about a viper who lives in Stillwood Heights. Something about a disagreement while you and Renton were visiting, and a misunderstanding ensued."

The bobcat I'd called Hemingway glanced at me. "Sorry, I've never seen him before."

Ward waved away the feline's denial. "Mr. Anoraq isn't interested in any misunderstandings, but he would like to have someone accompany him to Stillwood Heights. I understand it's not within our jurisdiction, and legally there's nothing we can do. But I thought of you. Someone who would make sure that Mr. Anoraq would not be detoured from getting the information he needs. Think of it as a personal favor for a very prominent friend."

The bobcat glanced from Ward to me and back again.

"When do we go?"

"Now's fine with me," I said.

Petoskey nodded, and Ward smiled. "Wonderful. Petoskey will take care of you, Mr. Anoraq. He's a fine officer."

"You've been very helpful, chief. I can't thank you enough," I said and shook his hand.

The bobcat and I left the chief's office, and we were halfway down the hall before he turned to me and said, "You played that smart. What's your game?"

CHAPTER 33

Petoskey drove the car while I gazed out at the house we passed.

"What did you tell him?" he asked.

"Not much, I left out the part about Dr. Winkler."

"What for?"

"Because I wanted your cooperation."

The bobcat's face scrunched up in a frown. "Do you really want to go over to Stillwood Heights?"

"No, how's your buddy Renton?"

"That grouse is in the hospital."

The news surprised me, and I gave Petoskey a questioning glance.

"He wasn't shot. Something to do with his innards. The bird was in a lot of pain before he went into the hospital, and now he might not come out."

"Karma," I said. "You don't seem too concerned."

"I'm not. That birds a piece of work. It was his idea to hand you over to the doc. I wanted to leave you close to the nearest taxi stand. Renton, he's got it in for all meat eaters. He enjoyed playing with you. Since the bird outranks me, what could I do? Dr. Winkler was his idea."

"Did Dalimil know you took me over to that place?"

The bobcat shrugged, "I don't think so, but Renton was chummy with that viper, not me. How much trouble am I in?"

"That depends on how cooperative you are. I didn't walk into Chief Ward's office without credentials."

"Okay."

"So why was I shot full of drugs and placed on a forty-eight-hour lockdown in the dear doctor's care?"

Petoskey pulled the car to the curb, and we waited for the telogen hairs that shot out of his fur to settle or blow away. I stuck my head out the window and sneezed.

The feline studied his claws. "I didn't know about that."

"Everything was on me, keys, identification, money, and such. Winkler knew you guys too well to think I was a gag, so I'm curious."

"It's safer not to be. Did you bring the Los Angeles males in on this?"

"Not really, though I do have a few contacts and a friend in the D.A.'s office. The only reason I haven't dropped in on him is that this is a private job. I am a private investigator after all."

"So what are you really after?" he asked.

"What's Dr. Winkler's real job?"

Petoskey tapped the steering wheel with his claws. "Most cops don't get paid much, but neither do we go bad for money. Most of us just do what we're told, and the next thing we know we're up to our necks in the kind of trouble we can't get out of. If either Renton or I knew what Dr. Winkler was really up too, we wouldn't have dumped you there."

"Are you so sure about Renton?"

The big cat thought for a bit. "Yeah, the bird liked dishing it out, but not taking it."

"What if I told you that I suspect the dear doctor of using scopolamine on me? A truth serum to make me talk. The stuff works better than hypnotism, but not by much. The only reason for the mouse to do that was if someone told him. That narrows it down to Dalimil, Big Kelly, or police gag."

His ears moved forward as he looked at me. "Who's Big Kelly?"

"A very large hippo who killed a lizard, and beat up

another, over on Central Avenue a few days ago. If you read your teletype you'd know about it. Dr. Winkler was hiding the hippo in his private hospital, and I spotted the big male before I left the place. The male had all the comforts of home."

"Did he spot you?"

"Not on my way out."

Petoskey put the car in gear and pulled away from the curb. "Let's check it out. Here I thought the guy just peddled dope. Small time. Never thought of him hiding crooks."

"The numbers racket can be small time, but when you put all the bingo halls and gambling parlors together, it can get pretty big."

The feline frowned but didn't bite. He drove towards Dr. Winkler's place, slowed down when we came near but didn't stop. The building and yard looked cheerful in the daylight. "Someone knows about the doc. The rodent near the palm tree was a Los Angeles cop. The chief will flip out about them coming to town uninvited."

"Is there a connection between Dalimil and Winkler?"

"None that I know of."

"Do you know who runs this town?"

"That's common knowledge."

"Mike Castle?" When the bobcat nodded, I asked, "Where can I find him?"

"How the hell should I know? The skunk could be in Mexico for all I care."

"Okay, do you mind dropping me back off downtown?"

"Sure."

Petoskey drove back to City Hall and parked. Before I got out of the vehicle, he said, "Castle owns two gambling ships out in the bay. They're supposed to be outside city and state jurisdiction."

CHAPTER 34

The waterfront hotel I decided to stay at didn't have the softest mattress in the world, but it worked. The glare of the neon sign outside the window was the same. When the room glowed red, it would be time for me to leave. In the meantime, I let my mind go over everything that had happened in the last few days, the connections and the people involved.

When it was time, I got up, washed my face, and stepped out of the room. On my way out of the hotel, I dropped the key to the room at the desk and tried not to think about there not being a return trip.

People were everywhere. The bingo parlor was full, sailors walked with their arms around their sweethearts, and a sausage vendor barked his wares at the passing crowd.

I walked in one direction, meandering along the sidewalk until I could smell more sea air than frying fat and butter laden popcorn. A sidewalk car buzzed along the wide walkway, and I hopped a ride, all the while looking for a tail. I didn't see any.

The dachshund selling sausages looked like he was doing a good business, and I walked over.

"What's the name of the boats out there?" I asked, interrupting his barking.

"The Monte Carlo and the Belterra."

"What's the difference between them?"

The dog looked at me, but a customer kept him from answering until food and money changed hands.

"They both have gambling."

"Is one further out then the other?"

He gave me the once over and said, "You look like a cop."

"Private." I paid for a sausage with all the trimmings and gave him a tip.

"The Belterra is for the nice people just out for some fun. That's the closer one. The Monte Carlo is the one you're probably curious about and is out further." The dog looked me up and down again. "Better learn how to swim before you go."

I nodded my thanks and ate my sausage. It was good, and a lot better than the lunch I'd had earlier that tasted more like cardboard with tomato sauce. Looking around, I still couldn't see anyone following me, so I stopped in a bar for a drink and to ease my nerves.

CHAPTER 35

Three couples rode with me on the water taxi out to the boat. Three sides of the craft were glassed in to enjoy the view, but nobody was interested. They were too busy playing kissy face with each other. The ride was long, but the dark waters made it seem longer, especially when the swells hit the boat and bounced us around.

The walrus manning the boat wasn't bothered by the waters, but he wouldn't be. The passengers were more likely to give him problems, and that was probably why he wore a black leather hip-holster.

As more water came between the boat and the lights of Bay City, the more my dinner wanted to make a return visit.

The lights of the Belterra loomed into view but we didn't stop. The Monte Carlo was our destination. The smaller boat snuck out of the darkness, and unlike the Belterra's flash and glitz, the Monte Carlo looked like and old maid. The darkness prevented me from seeing the rust on the hull, but I had no doubt the converted freighter was covered in it. The music was the same as the Belterra, but the lighting wasn't nearly as bright.

The water taxi made a wide sweeping turn before easing up to the hemp fenders along the docking stage. While the engine of the taxi idled, a lone searchlight from the freighter scanned the waters about fifty yards out.

The walrus hooked the taxi to the stage as a blue jacketed otter helped the passengers off the taxi. I was the last one off, but when the guy casually bumped into me, he stopped smiling.

"Guns aren't allowed." He signaled the walrus, and the guy came out of the boat to stand behind me.

"Would you like me to check it? I'm here to see Castle on business."

"Castle who?" sneered the otter. "Now beat it."

When I tried to argue, the walrus picked me up and dropped me back into the taxi. "This is not the place you want to argue with people. So unless you want to dog paddle back to shore, shut up." The taxi rocked so much as the walrus got back in that I couldn't stand and ended up tumbling into a seat. I stayed there until we reached the shore. The walrus didn't pay me any more attention other than to give me back my quarter for the ride as I stepped onto the dock.

I stepped past the people getting onto the taxi and made my way back to the sand. The dark almond eyes of a big malamute in a torn sailor's shirt twinkled as he smiled at me. "Did St. Peter send you back?"

"Go mend your shirt."

"That gun of yours is a little obvious under such a light suit."

"What do you care?"

"I don't, just curious." He smiled a little wider and offered his hand. "Everyone calls me Frost."

As much as I was miffed about my plan not working, the big lug had the ability to take away the sting of failure. "Lucius Anoraq."

He looked at me sideways and asked, "Do you really want on that old freighter?"

"What'll it cost?"

"Fifty."

"Nice meeting you." I walked past the big male.

"Twenty-five then. Less if you bring friends."

"Friends are hard to find." I continued walking and made my way through the crowd. The bingo hall was still going strong, and I stopped to watch the flashing lights.

That's when the big fluffy shadow came up beside me. "Funds must be tight."

The malamute had nice markings with eyes so dark they were almost black. "You're not a regular cop, private detective, without an expense account?"

When I didn't say anything, Frost kept talking. "Going in the front way wasn't a good idea. Not unless you just wanted to gamble. Otherwise those mugs out there would play for keeps. That's international waters out there, it may as well be the wilderness."

"Mind telling me what kind of racket you're running?"

"A little of this and a little of that. I used to be on the police force but most of the honest cops were all pushed out, including me."

"Do you know about Mike Castle?"

His ears twitched as someone called bingo, but his eyes stayed on an eagle in a wrinkled suit as the bird stepped close to us. When the bird didn't move, Frost leaned over and asked, "Is there something I can do for you?"

The eagle smiled but went on his way.

"This is a good place to talk," said Frost. "People pay attention to the numbers, while anyone not looking are holding conversations or picking pockets. I've got a friend who'd be willing to lend me his boat. It's at the pier down the line. No lights. There's a loading port on the Monte Carlo I can access. In fact, I've been known to take a load out there from time to time. It helps that there isn't much in the way of crew below decks."

"What about the searchlights?"

"There's a lot of water to cover."

I didn't know what else to do, so I slipped a twenty and a five from my wallet and folded them into a small square. "One way?" I asked.

"Fifteen."

"Consider the rest a tip." The bills passed between us in a handshake, and the malamute disappeared in the crowd.

The eagle swung back around and asked, "The dog in the sailor shirt, he a friend of yours? He reminds me of someone."

Instead of answering, I walked out the doors and into the crowd outside. The eagle tried tailing me, so I double backed and came up beside him. "For a quarter I'll guess your weight." The gun he was packing wasn't that noticeable.

"Do I need to arrest someone? Maybe you or your friend?"

"Why would a cop have to arrest another cop?"

The bird blinked a couple times before deflating his feathers. "Damn, I thought that guy looked familiar." With his feathered tail low to the ground, the guy walked back the way he'd come.

CHAPTER 36

Beyond the sidewalk cars, the lights of the entertainment places, and the aroma of food, stood the darkened pier jutting out of the water.

Frost stood up, the white of his fur a ghostly glow. He didn't face me as he talked. "Go on to the sea steps, I'll get the boat."

"That eagle was a waterfront cop; I had a talk with him."

"Pickpocket detail. The bird's good, too good. Some poor suckers find extra wallets in their pockets when his arrest record dips."

"In other words, typical Bay City." I looked out onto the water. "Are you sure there will be enough fog to hide us from the searchlights?"

"And the tommy guns. Don't worry."

The malamute disappeared into the darkness, and I stepped out onto the fish-slimed planks to listen to the water against the piles.

The noise of the engine briefly carried over the water, then silence. Eventually, the boat slid up to the steps, and I climbed aboard, joining Frost under the screen. The angry burbling of the craft felt like the roar of Niagara Falls in my ears, but it didn't seem to faze Frost.

Once again, the lights of Bay City receded, and we passed the first boat before coming to the freighter. The cold finger of fear tightened my chest. "What if I don't find Castle? What if I drowned in the dark waters?"

"Nice pep talk. Castle could be anywhere. What are you

really looking for?"

"A hippo by the name of Big Kelly." I told Frost more. A lot more than I'd intended, but he was a good listener.

"Quite a puzzle," said Frost, when I finished. "This Dr. Winkler would have needed an in with the city, but that doesn't mean the city knew everything he was up to. Maybe Renton did, but I doubt Petoskey knew much. He's not the greatest cop, but he's not bad. As for the psychic, I can't figure how he fits in to all this. A diversion perhaps. Renton's the type to use anyone to his own advantage, and you would have been the perfect agent, so he could put a bigger squeeze on Dr. Winkler."

"So I'm chasing my tail?"

"I didn't say that." Frost scratched his chin. "Castle can't be bothered to run the town; he just wants his gambling establishments to make money and not be bothered. The skunk might know what's going on, but he wouldn't have anything to do with the jewel heist. Too petty. I'd say that's more likely to tie into Winkler."

"But a hound was murdered."

"Castle might have a guy killed, but you can be sure he wouldn't leave a body to be discovered. The skunk has brains, and he uses them. Killing is a last resort."

"So you're saying Castle wouldn't hide Big Kelly, particularly after the hippo killed two people?"

Frost nodded. "That's exactly what I'm saying. If Castle is hiding the guy, there's more to your case than money. Do you still want to board the freighter?"

"Yes."

CHAPTER 37

The searchlight swung lazily around. It was still early in the evening by gambling house standards. Any good hijacker would wait until later when the crowd dispersed and the workers were tired to pull anything.

We watched from beyond the reach of the searchlights as the water taxi dumped off its passengers. Frost maneuvered his boat in the water, and we slipped past everything right up to the hull of the freighter. The fog made everything unreal. I watched Frost work while the search lights panned out in the water.

An iron ladder was bolted close to the plates, and Frost hauled his large body up the rungs, leaving me at the wheel. I heard the faint creak of hinges and saw the outline of a loading port. Frost whistled, and I left the boat to climb onto the freighter. Frost made it look easy. I, on the other hand, tumbled over onto my rear into a bunch of packing boxes.

Frost stayed close, and his warm breath tickled my ear. "From here, it's a straight shot to the boiler room catwalk. They'll only have one male down here on account of the crew doubling as dealers. In the boiler room, there's a vent with no grate in it and goes all the way up on deck. Only the boat deck is off limits. Once there, you're on your own. Will you be coming back fast?"

"I'll probably make a nice splash from the boat deck."

Frost put his hand on my shoulder. "It's okay to be scared."

That's when I realized my ears were down, and my tail

was tucked between my legs. I tried loosening up and said, "Let's get this over with."

The only person we came across was a pelican dozing in a chair. Frost made sure he was knocked out and trussed up before we moved on. "Going up the ventilator, you'll make a lot of noise, but only those down here will hear you. Up top, it'll be nice and quiet."

"Guess this is goodbye," I said.

"If you need help, I could stay. You have no idea how much I hate these bastards."

"No, you've done enough. I should have paid you more."

"Don't worry about it. Get going. Stop by the bingo hall some time." Frost smiled, took a few steps, and came back. "Use the information about the open loading port if you have to. It could buy you your life."

CHAPTER 38

The climb up the ventilator seemed endless as cool air rushed down over me before I poked my nose out the horn at the top. A quick sniff told me no one was close, so I scurried out onto the deck as my ears heard everything from people talking to music. I pulled my gun from the shoulder holster and kept it close to my side.

I wasn't alone for long. An ox and a stag conversed farther on, but I couldn't hear what they were saying.

"The boat deck is off limits to guests." The voice came from behind me, and I turned slowly to find a skunk, his hands empty.

"I must have gotten lost," I said.

"You must have. The door at the bottom of the companionway is kept locked, but some people jump the chain on the stairway."

"Someone must have left the door open."

"Were you part of a party?"

"Turn your head and someone else is buying them a drink."

He nodded, and I dropped, rolled, avoiding the blackjack, and came up with my gun ready. "Don't be heroes, I'd rather not make a lot of noise."

The ox with the blackjack didn't move. But while neither did the skunk, he did talk. "You do realize, you'll never leave this boat."

"I've been thinking of that, but if you don't mind, I'd like to talk to Mike Castle."

"He's in San Diego."

105

"His stand in will do."

The skunk looked at the ox, and he waved him away before turning back to me. "This way, and put the heater away, please."

He led me down a set of stairs and through what I first thought was a locked door. Once inside, I holstered my gun. A gilded arch led into a gaming room where about sixty people were gambling on everything from faro to roulette.

Two boars in dinner jackets passed us by and acted like they meant to pull out their cigarette cases. I was flanked.

"You're Castle, aren't you?" I asked.

"Yes, this way please."

All four of us walked into another room. From the bunks, booze, magazines, and cigarettes the place was used by the crew to relax in.

"Relieve him of his gun for the time being, please."

I didn't resist when one of the boars opened my jacket to take the thing and drop it on the desk. He stationed himself beside the door and the other left.

Castle offered me a drink, and we both sat down with a glass of scotch and a lit cigarette.

When the boar who'd left returned, it was with the otter from the taxi drop off. The male's mouth dropped open, and he pointed at me. "He didn't get past me; I know he didn't."

"He had this on him." Castle pointed at my gun. "It was rather disconcerting to have it pointed at me."

The pair bickered back and forth, with the otter denying everything. In the end the otter attempted to take a swing at me, but the boar that brought him into the room clocked him first, knocking him out.

The skunk looked at me. "There's still the question of how you got up on deck. Who are you?"

"Lucius Anoraq, I'm a private detective, and I'd like to talk to a hippo named Big Kelly." I showed him my ID on request, and after looking at it, he tossed it back. "I'm investigating the murder of a hound named Cedrick Brinkman. It happened Thursday near one of your clubs. The hound's murder also connects to two other murders done by a bank robber named Big Kelly."

"I'm assuming you'll eventually get to the point, but the only thing I'm interested in is how you got onto my boat. I know you didn't get past the otter at the taxi drop off. I choose my crew very carefully."

"Listen, I know you own a good chunk of Bay City, maybe all of it. I don't care. What I do know is a mouse by the name of Dr. Winkler was hiding Big Kelly and peddling dope on the side. Maybe he did a few other things as well. The doctor wouldn't be able to do anything without your protection. Now Winkler moved his operation, and Big Kelly is hiding somewhere else."

"And you think this Big Kelly is here?" he asked.

"Not really. I was more hoping you'd help me out."

The skunk's tail twitched, the only sign of his emotions. "Tell me how you got on my ship?"

"Do I have to?"

"Yes." He flicked his tail again.

"If I tell you, will you get in touch with Big Kelly?" When he raised an eyebrow, I pulled out one of my cards and wrote a few cryptic words on the back. "This should do."

The skunk picked up the card, read what I wrote, and said, "Meaningless."

"To you, but not Big Kelly."

"You're an odd one. Why go through all this trouble?" The way the skunk acted, I wasn't sure if he knew a thing about the hippo.

I nodded. "On the first trip out, I made a big mistake with the gun. My bad. Then I met someone willing to help me on the beach." A flicker of anger passed over his face, and I hoped I hadn't just dropped Frost into the deep end. "The guy wasn't a crook, just someone who listened and listened good. He heard about the unbarred loading port, a ventilator shaft with no grate, and only one guy to knock out."

Castle signaled one of the boars to go checkout what I said. When he left, the skunk chuckled and pushed my gun toward me. "It's certainly been an interesting night. If I can find this, Big Kelly, I'll give him your message, but he isn't here, and I don't know him."

"Thanks."

After the boar came back and confirmed my story, Castle and I shook hands, he gave me another drink and let me go. No one bothered me, but I still didn't rest easy until the water taxi dropped me back off on land.

I went back to the bingo parlor and within a few minutes Frost was at my side. "You survived."

"If it wasn't for you, I'd be drowned."

"What about your hippo?"

"No dice, but Castle's worried, I think. With any luck, he'll find him for me."

The eagle walked by us again, and Frost elbowed him on his way out of the bingo hall. I wanted to clock the eagle myself but figured I couldn't risk spending any more time in Bay City tonight. Once Frost left, there was nothing left for me to do but go home, sleep, and wait.

CHAPTER 39

Around ten o'clock, I called Athena Anne French and caught her before she headed out for the night.

"I promised to call you, though I'm sorry about the lateness of the hour," I said.

"Are you standing me up again?"

"Depends. If the chauffeur works late, he can pick me up. I still need to crawl into my suit."

"Should I bother?"

"I'll show you my etching."

"Only one?" she asked.

"It's a small apartment."

"Stop playing hard to get and give me your address."

After I gave her the address, I told her about the lobby being locked and that I'd go down and slip the catch. I did just that after hanging up, then took a shower. Instead of getting dressed, I put on my pajamas and laid down on the bed. I was out before I knew it.

Something woke me, a sound or smell, and I almost rolled over and ignored it I was so tired. But the smell of male and gun oil had my eyes popping open. Big Kelly sat in one of my chairs, but his sheer size shrunk my apartment.

I shifted to a sitting position and rubbed the sleep out of my eyes. "I was hoping you'd stop by. Don't' worry, there's no cops around."

"You expecting someone besides me?"

"Just a dame. I didn't mean to fall asleep.

Big Kelly's ears moved like spinning tops before

settling back into place. The gun in his hand still looked like a toy. "Why'd you think I was on the Monte Carlo?"

"Just something someone said. Doesn't matter. You made a bit of a mess when you killed Ginger Bloom. I understand that was a mistake. You don't know your own strength, but I understand how much it upset you not to have the answers you were looking for."

The big hippo shifted in the chair. Though it creaked in protest, the chair held.

"When I found her, a cop was with me," I said. "Sorry, but I had to tell him what I knew. What I knew at the time at least."

"She didn't tell me about Jade."

"The rat didn't know. Jade was too smart for her."

The hippo's forehead wrinkled as he frowned. "How'd you find out I was on the boat?"

"That was guesswork, really. I see Castle gave you my message."

"Yeah. Never met the guy, but he seems nice from what I've heard. When do we do what you said on the card?"

"Soon."

Before I could elaborate, the door handle to the apartment rattled. Both of us stood, but I held up my hand in hopes he'd listen to me and stay calm, and I yelled, "Who is it?"

"The Queen of England, who do you think?"

I waved Big Kelly toward the dressing room and hissed, "It's the dame. Hide in there until I can get rid of her."

The expression on the big hippo's face was unreadable, but he picked up his hat and squeezed into the small room shutting the door as far as it would go, leaving a good one-inch gap.

I grabbed my robe, put it on and flipped the catch on the door. Big Kelly must have put it back on when he came into my apartment.

When I opened the door, Athena French's sultry smile turned cold as she looked me up and down. Dressed in emeralds and wearing an outfit that molded to her body, she was ready for whatever the night had in store. She wasn't happy with my pajamas.

"Are you serious?" she asked.

"Sorry, a cop stopped by and, well you know how they are."

"Hartman?"

I smiled, nodded, and stepped aside. The vixen hesitated a minute before entering my apartment in a cloud of expensive perfume. "Let's get one thing straight, I don't do back door anything. I've come up in the world and don't have to deal with that kind of stuff anymore."

"If you're planning on leaving, would you like a drink first?"

"I'm not leaving, just making a point. What do you have to drink?"

"Nothing as high-end as you're used to, I expect, but hopefully it's palatable."

I slipped into the kitchen, made the drinks, and came out with two glasses.

Athena French took hers, sipped, and looked me over again. "To bad you met me at the door in your pajamas. I rather liked you. Big, strong, and blue eyes. I bet you have a lot of muscle underneath all that fur."

"I've got a few."

She pulled a cigarette out of her purse, and I lit it for her before we both sat down.

"Why don't we talk?"

"About my jade necklace?"

"I was thinking more along the lines of murder."

"Do we have to? Cedrick Brinkman wasn't a saint, but the subject of his murder is so dreary."

"The dog wasn't a spotter for jewel thieves, was he? Probably not much of a blackmailer either. No, you still have your necklace in some vault somewhere."

"Really?" Her eyes narrowed, as she set her drink on the nearest table.

I downed my own drink. "Seeing as the necklace was never stolen, that means there is no gang. So why was Brinkman murdered? Was it because he didn't have what it takes to kill someone? Someone like me?"

The change in her was eerie along with being quick. The vixen no longer looked beautiful but more like a Hollywood cutout. "What an interesting thought. Does someone hate you that much?"

"Probably."

"Where's your proof?"

"That's the crux isn't it? A convicted crook gets out of the joint, and the only thing he wants to do is find his old flame. A torch singer. I get curious, so it looks like I'm helping the guy. Must not have been too hard, because Brickman didn't take much convincing that I had to go. Only he didn't have the stomach for killing, or at least didn't like the risk involved. The problem was that he didn't want to lose his meal ticket."

"It's an interesting story." The cigarette in her hand was forgotten but kept burning.

"Why don't we stop running around the bush, we're alone here. You're a poor female who made good and married a multimillionaire. An old rat recognized you by your voice I'm guessing. She liked to listen to the radio a lot. You were able to pay her off and cheaply, so I gather she didn't realize who you married, only that you did well for yourself. Brickman was just the go between, the rat's handler, so to speak. That's why the trust deed. The thought of getting tossed out on the street kept her in line."

I paused, lit my own cigarette, and gauged the vixen's mood. She remained stone cold silent.

"But Big Kelly was out of jail and wanted to find his female because he loved her, and a lug like me got curious. Brinkman became a liability. You let your frustrations out on him with a sap."

Mrs. Athena Anne French didn't scream or growl. She just dropped her burnt out cigarette on my floor and calmly pulled a gun out of her purse.

She would have kept that calm had Big Kelly not busted out of my dressing room still holding his own gun. "I'd know that voice anywhere, Jade. Heard it for years. You look good, though I like the red fur better."

The fur on her back rose and her tail bristled as she jumped from the chair, pointing the gun at him. With ears flattened to her head she screamed, "Stay away from me."

Big Kelly stopped moving, he didn't raise the gun, it stayed forgotten in his hand. It was the brain behind the not so intelligent eyes that managed to put the pieces together, and it showed on his face. "You turned me in. Why Jade?"

Her answer was five bullets in his gut. Lucky for me because when she turned the gun on me, the thing was empty. We both made a dive for Big Kelly's gun, but I got there first. When she bolted for the door, I let her go and checked Big Kelly. The big hippo was alive, but by the look on his face, he wished he wasn't.

I telephoned the Receiving Hospital before calling Hartman. "You're not going to believe this, but Big Kelly is in my apartment. Mrs. Athena Anne French emptied her gun into his gut and ran."

"You just had to play it clever didn't you, Anoraq?"

It took a couple of oxen to get the hippo on the stretcher and out the door. The canary was optimistic about saving him and thought the hippo had a chance.

Big Kelly didn't want it and died that night.

CHAPTER 40

"Why didn't you have a dinner party and reveal all?" asked Mary Abrams. She tasted her drink and sat down. "It could have been all Agatha Christie."

"Real life isn't scripted, and you don't get second takes."

"Too bad she got away."

The drink she'd fixed me was on the weak side but wasn't bad. "Athena French must have had a bolt hole because she never went home. She drove her own car to my place, so she didn't have to worry about what to do with a chauffeur, and who knows what she stored in the trunk."

"Will they bother to try to catch her?"

"D.A. Marvin Penner is a good fox and a straight shooter. I used to work for him. Granted, it'll be next to impossible to prove she killed Brinkman even without her pretty face and money. She's got no record. As for her shooting Big Kelly, the hippo had a gun."

The Irish Setter shook her head, setting her red curls bouncing. "If you'd have told me about him, I could have figured everything out for you. Those two pictures didn't even match. They weren't the same vixen."

"I know. I'm not sure why Mrs. Bloom kept a photo with the wrong name on it. Maybe Brinkman switched the thing. That's something we'll never know. It was her voice that gave the vixen away. All I know for sure is that when I contacted the rat, looking for Jade, she called Brinkman. The hound then called me with the jewel heist lie. If they hadn't of panicked, everything would have blown over."

"Why didn't Mrs. Bloom ask for more money?"

"I doubt if she knew Jade's real name or remembered what she looked like. As I said, it was her voice that gave her away. Mrs. Bloom was still a liability, and if Big Kelly hadn't killed her, the vixen would have."

Mary sat her drink down. "Poor Mr. French."

"Poor Mr. French, my eye. That old fox isn't cooperating with the police at all. The old tod is still in love with his wife even with the way she treated him."

"I bet she treated you nice."

"She was scared of me and tried playing me. Only she didn't realize I couldn't be played that way." I looked down at my empty glass, but Mary didn't take the hint.

"The female played every male she ever met. Did she have her hooks in Winkler, Dalimil, Castle?"

"Turns out Dalimil's wanted by Scotland Yard. The viper was just a con artist. They picked him up in a hotel in Paris, but he had nothing to do with the case. I'm not sure about Dr. Winkler, but they haven't been able to track him down yet. As for Castle, he's spotless, and his lawyers will make sure no one touches him. I'm surprised he's letting Bay City get cleaned up. What cops haven't been let go have been busted down to beat cops. But I am glad that Frost got his job back."

The thought of the malamute had my mind wandering, and I missed the next few sentences Mary said until she poked me.

"Are you listening to me?"

"What?"

"I said you're wonderful and asked why you haven't tried to kiss me."

"Oh, about that, let me explain."

CHAPTER 41

The police didn't find Mrs. French AKA Jade until three months later. Part of the reason was that she stayed away from the moneyed crowd and went back to her roots and into the clubs.

A Baltimore cop with a conductor's ear and perfect pitch wandered into the right gin joint. The vixen had changed her markings again and dyed her fur black, but her voice gave her away, again.

Supposedly, the cop entered her dressing room with the wanted poster, and instead of arresting her, the male ended up shot to pieces.

"She committed suicide," said Hartman. The armadillo munched on an ant cake while I snacked on a handful of kibble.

"With two bullets in her chest?"

"The coroner said something about reflex shot, but since I wasn't there and didn't see it with my own eyes, I won't comment. Drugs were involved, I'm told."

"She could have tried playing the cop and everything went wrong."

"Possible, but I'd hate to think that way." Hartman tossed the remains of the ant cake on a plate. "If she would have given herself up, she could have got off scot free. With her looks and money, the lawyers could have spun a poor female makes good, but the leeches in her life wouldn't let her be, story."

"Maybe she did it for the old tod? Maybe she really

loved her husband and didn't want to have him embarrassed by everything that would come out?"

"It's a nice thought. Do you really believe it?"

I didn't answer. I just looked out the window at the cool clear day.

COLLECT ALL THE POACHED PARODIES BOOKS

THE LIZARD FIFTH
Scarlet Crop
The Lamarre Curse
The Persian Penguin
The Crystal Screw
The Lean Male

KAISER WRENCH
I, the Tribunal
My Claws are Quick
Retribution is Mine!
A Solitary Evening
The Great Slay
Pet Me Fatal
The Female Trackers
The Worm
The Contorted Figure
The Figure Fans
Existence…Eliminated
The Carnage Male
Dark Lane

LUCIUS ANORAQ
The Long Slumber
Goodbye Gorgeous
The Lofty Perch
The Female in the Water
The Wee Sibling
The Lengthy Farewell
Recap

For more information go to www.stacybender.net

Made in the USA
Columbia, SC
10 July 2023

20017613R00074